WHO GETS THE APARTMENT?

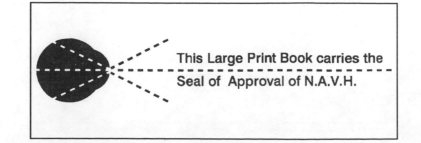

This Large Print Book carries the
Seal of Approval of N.A.V.H.

WHO GETS THE APARTMENT?

STEVEN RIGOLOSI

THORNDIKE PRESS

An imprint of Thomson Gale, a part of The Thomson Corporation

THOMSON

GALE

Detroit • New York • San Francisco • New Haven, Conn. • Waterville, Maine • London

THOMSON
———✳———™
GALE

LIBRARY OF CONGRESS CATALOGING-IN-PUBLICATION DATA

Rigolosi, Steven A.
  Who gets the apartment? / by Steven Rigolosi.
    p. cm. — (Tales from the back page ; #1) (Thorndike Press large print clean reads)
  ISBN 0-7862-9040-4 (alk. paper)
    1. Apartment dwellers — Fiction. 2. Manhattan (New York, N.Y.) — Fiction. 3. Book editors — Fiction. 4. Large type books. I. Title.
  PS3618.I43W48 2006b
  813'.6—dc22   2006023166

U.S. Hardcover:
ISBN 13: 978-0-7862-9040-6
ISBN 10: 0-7862-9040-4

Published in 2006 by arrangement with Ransom Note Press.

Printed in the United States of America on permanent paper
10 9 8 7 6 5 4 3 2 1

Dedicated with gratitude and respect to
Marc Lieberman
and
Lorraine Patsco

CONTENTS

■ ■ ■ ■

WHO GETS THE APARTMENT?

■ ■ ■ ■

The ad. That's how it all started.

For a few weeks I felt as if I'd won the lottery. I had visions of a bright future in my luxurious penthouse apartment, where I'd host book discussion groups during the week and cocktail parties on the weekends. A place

11

where I could have both a bedroom *and* an office, not a tiny studio so crammed with books and junk that a misplaced cigarette would have sent the entire building up in flames. A welcoming haven for friends from college and visitors from abroad.

Looking back now, I wonder how we all could have been so naïve.

I've learned a few lessons, though. Things don't always go according to plan, and any crisis can have an infinite variety of outcomes, depending on the people involved and their moods at the time. When I moved into Apartment 18D, I had no premonition that three years later I'd be sitting here in Greenwich Village, embarking on a new career after two unexpected adventures.

And speaking of adventures . . . Since I didn't know what would happen to me, why should you? I didn't know where I would end up, so why should I spoil the surprise by telling you how I got there, without first teasing you a little bit, the same way fate teased me? So please don't complain if I give you four possible options and let you figure out which one really happened. You've been warned.

— C.J.

■ ■ ■ ■

THE ARRIVAL OF
LADY LUCK

■ ■ ■ ■

1

Anyone who's sought a decent apartment at a decent price in a decent Manhattan neighborhood knows that you need only one thing to find such a place: sheer, unadulterated, God-sent good luck.

With waiting lists for rent-controlled buildings reaching the 15-year mark, some enterprising Manhattanites have developed creative methods of apartment hunting. They rise early to scan the obituaries, then arrive at the buildings of the recently deceased with pocketfuls of cash, hoping to cajole the building manager into giving them the recently vacated apartment. They marry or declare domestic partnerships with complete strangers to get their name on a lease. They chase down every possible lead generated by friends, family, and co-workers. But none of these methods work unless Lady Luck is firmly on their side. And today, for some happy reason, she smiled on Corinne Jensen.

Corinne had had a terrible night's sleep — if you could call tossing, turning, sweating, and semiconscious hallucinating a "night's sleep." It was rumored that her company might be put up for sale, and she wondered if she'd survive yet another horrible merger or acquisition. Her Mom and Dad, back in Buffalo, seemed to be going downhill, and she knew that sooner or later she'd have to start sending money. She didn't resent this (it was only fair, since her sister had the far more onerous task of actually caring for their parents), but it wasn't as though New York book editors had a lot of extra cash lying around.

But these worries paled in comparison to the prospect of being thrown out of her apartment, which was imminent. The building was going co-op and she didn't have the money for a down payment. She *should* have saved more. But it's impossible to save money when you live in Manhattan. Everyone knows that.

She'd spent the last three months in a fruitless quest for something she could afford and feel safe in. All she wanted was a simple one-bedroom apartment, like her current place, but even small studios on the Upper West Side were renting for eight or nine hundred dollars more than her small, pleasant apartment on 88th Street.

All her problems would have been solved if she'd been willing to relocate to, say, Brooklyn. But the Upper West Side, where she'd lived since coming to New York after college, was her *home*. She knew the cashiers at Zabar's by name. The brothers who ran the newsstand on Amsterdam Avenue taught her a new Russian word each time she picked up the new *Vogue*. She even had "her" table at Café 82, a small diner on Broadway.

She looked at the clock: 5:09 a.m. She groaned and gave up any hope of sleep. She might as well get up and go for a run.

The morning was crisp and chilly. She felt invigorated as she stepped out of the building and began a slow jog. As she ran, she tried to block out the feelings of envy she felt for the residents of each and every apartment building on West End Avenue. *All those people,* she thought, torturing herself, *cuddled up in their beds, sleeping like babies, not about to be kicked out onto the street.*

As she ran in place, waiting for a traffic signal to change, a delivery truck for *The Clarion* pulled alongside her. A burly man tossed two bundles of the new issue onto the curb, then climbed out to stuff the newspapers into the yellow box from which neighborhood residents could retrieve their free copies.

Corinne loved *The Clarion.* It billed itself, somewhat pretentiously, as "the voice of the Upper West Side." Full of attitude and opinions, the paper was heavy on coverage of cultural events and local politics.

When the driver pulled away, she opened the box and took out a copy. The driver had stuffed the papers into the box upside down, so the first thing she saw was the "Clarion Bulletin Board" on the back page.

The ad leapt off the page:

FOR RENT

Central Park West & 72nd Street. Luxurious 3000 sq ft. duplex penthouse: 2 bedrooms, fireplaces in LR & master BR, 3 baths, cathedral ceilings, all modern kitchen with DW & all new appliances, dining room, balcony overlooking the park, doorman bldg with full security features, basement parking included. $600/month. Two-year lease. Available first of the month. Call 212-555-2997.

$600 a month? Impossible. Surely they

meant $6,000? But . . . what if she really could get an apartment ten times the size of her current place for a third of what she was currently paying?

She looked at her watch: 5:36. It was probably too early to call the number, but she didn't care. She ran to the public phone at the other end of the block, praying that, just once, some stupid kid hadn't smashed the receiver or used his pocketknife to cut the wires. Miracle of miracles — she picked up the receiver and got a dial tone. She punched in her calling card number (which she'd long ago committed to memory) and the number listed in the ad. After two rings, a male voice said "Hello."

"Hi, I hope I'm not calling too early? My name's Corinne Jensen. I'm calling about the ad in *The Clarion*. Is the apartment on 72nd and Central Park West still available?"

"Yes, it is." The man sounded quite pleasant.

"Is the rent $600 a month?"

"Yes, that's correct."

"I'll take it."

There was a light chuckle. "Don't you want to see it first?"

"No. I'll take it."

"Miss — Jensen, did you say? — I can't rent an apartment to you over the phone.

We need to meet in person. Plus, I have to do credit checks, background checks, et cetera."

"Please don't give it to anyone else. I'll be right over. It's not too early to come, is it?"

"You can stop by any time. I'll be here all day, until about six. Let me give you the address." And he did.

"Please, please, don't give it to anyone else before I get there."

"Listen, I can't promise you anything. I'm only the rental agent. Just get here as soon as you can. And bring three months' rent and two months' security in cash, just in case."

"I'll be there within half an hour. Even if I have to steal a car. Who should I ask for at the building?"

"I'm Andrew Weisch. Have the doorman send you to Apartment 18D."

"I'm Corinne Jensen. Wait, I told you that already. OK, I'm hanging up now. I'll be there in half an hour. Bye."

She slammed the phone down and ran back to her apartment at cheetah-like speed. Good thing she'd decided to hide a substantial wad of hundred-dollar bills in her cookie jar! Manhattan landlords usually require security deposits in cash, and she hadn't wanted to find an acceptable apartment on an evening or weekend, then lose it to a rival renter because the banks were closed and ATM machines have a ridiculously small cash withdrawal limit. She smashed into the apartment, grabbed her nest egg, and ran back out the door without locking it. Back on Broadway, she hailed a taxi like a woman possessed.

She gave the address and held a twenty-dollar bill through the security window. "Get me there in under 10 minutes and this is your tip," she said, as if the cabbie needed an excuse to race through the streets of upper Manhattan like Jeff Gordon at the Daytona 500.

When the cab pulled up outside the building, a pristine pre-war high rise on the corner of Central Park West, Corinne threw the fare at the driver and raced into the lobby. She gave her name to the doorman, who sent her up to apartment 18D.

From the elevator, she could see Andrew Weisch waiting at the apartment door. He was tall, slender, and goodlooking, with a fashionable haircut and expensive designer eyeglasses and shoes. She forced herself to calm down and walk slowly.

"Mr. Weisch? Corinne Jensen. Sorry about the way I'm dressed. I was out jogging when I saw the ad, and I didn't want to waste any time in getting here. I really am a present-able person — I'm a book editor at Clarendon & Shaw."

Weisch smiled. "I don't usually look my best first thing in the morning, either. Come on in."

Corinne crossed the threshold and entered — a palace. She gasped as she surveyed the huge, open, L-shaped living room/dining room combination surrounded on two sides by floor-to-ceiling windows and a wrap-around balcony. A baby grand piano sat majestically off to one side. Corinne stared in slack-jawed amazement as Mr. Weisch led her through the dining room into the large eat-in kitchen, which was filled with expensive appliances and every modern convenience.

She continued to make small noises of wonder and astonishment as she followed Weisch up the stairs to the two bedrooms, both of which were larger than her entire apartment. The master bath had separate bathtub and shower stalls, a double sink, a skylight, a toilet, and a bidet. The second bedroom was only marginally smaller; the current resident seemed to use it as some sort of office. Both rooms had the same magnificent floor-to-ceiling windows and skylights.

Corinne was shaking with excitement. At the completion of the tour, she said with as much *sang froid* as she could muster, "This is certainly a lovely place. I'll take it."

"It *is* a wonderful apartment," Weisch admitted. "Let's get the applications taken care of." Corinne followed Weisch down the stairs like an obedient puppy.

"I need to make a few calls to check your employment status, credit rating, et cetera," Weisch said as she began filling out the paperwork. "Would you excuse me for a few minutes?"

"Of course," Corinne replied, fighting back a surge of optimism — as, she'd found, it never does pay to get one's hopes up. Still, she thought with some satisfaction, her credit was excellent, and she'd been with the same company for more than ten years.

She glanced at her watch. It was just after 6:30. "Isn't it too early to make business calls?" she asked.

"The agencies are open 24/7," Weisch replied, handing her a box of donuts. "Help yourself. I'll be back in a few."

She slowly munched on a half-stale cruller, nearly overwhelmed with excitement and joy. She envisioned the many fabulous wine-and-cheese parties she'd be hosting. And the thrill of having that second bedroom, for guests and for her computer . . . !

Weisch returned ten minutes later.

"Congratulations. The apartment's yours. As soon as you give me the first three months' rent and two months' security, of course."

Mr. Weisch outlined the tenant's guidelines as Corinne counted out the cash. "The apartment is rented unfurnished, so everything you see will be gone by the time you move in. The building has a zero-tolerance policy for pets, so I strongly advise you not to even *consider* sneaking one in. There's additional storage in the basement, in the cage marked 18D. The rent includes all utilities; we also arrange for your phone service, so you don't need to contact the phone company. Parties are allowed, but the building has strict policies about loudness after midnight.

"Do you have a car? No? OK, we'll rent the parking spot in the garage to someone else then. If you ever *do* get a car, let us know, and we'll see what we can do. But we can't *guarantee* a place in the garage.

"We expect the rent to be paid promptly on the first of each month. You can leave a check with the doorman, or I'll give you an address to send the check to.

"All these rules are spelled out in the

rental agreement," Weisch concluded, handing her three copies of that document to sign. "And that's the end of my spiel. Do you have any questions about the apartment or the building?"

"Just one. I don't mean to look a gift horse in the mouth, but why are you renting this place for such a . . . um. . . . reasonable price?"

Weisch shrugged his shoulders. "I wish I knew. This apartment's owned by the man I work for, John Blackmore. I just do what he tells me to do. He doesn't like his underlings asking him questions."

"Don't get me wrong, I'm not complaining. I was just wondering."

"The wealthy have their own way of doing things. I just go with the flow. Mine is not to question why, mine is just to do or die, blah blah blah."

She read over the terms of the rental agreement carefully. Nothing out of the ordinary. She'd never been happier to sign a document in her life.

Andrew Weisch also signed the agreement, then reached into his pocket and pulled out three sets of keys, which he dropped into Corinne's hand.

"Mr. Blackmore will countersign the agreement, and we'll FedEx a fully executed copy to your current address," Weisch said. "Give it a couple of days. Welcome to the building. You move in on the first."

2

Moving was a full-time job, no doubt about it. The utilities in the 88th Street apartment had to be shut off. Thousands of books had to be dusted and packed. The basement storage bin had to be cleaned out, credit card companies and magazine publishers had to be notified, movers had to be hired.

She didn't go into detail about the new place in conversations with friends, family, and co-workers. She simply mentioned that she'd found a "nice place in the low 70s," which seemed to satisfy everyone. She didn't consider herself a superstitious person, but she didn't want to jinx herself. Gushing about the ridiculously cheap duplex penthouse on Central Park West could only have resulted in some sort of cosmic revenge in which she'd lose the apartment.

She'd decided to take three vacation days — one for the move, one to unpack, and one to luxuriate in the comforts of Apartment 18D. The move went as well as an intra-Manhattan move can go. The movers were two hours late, and they came very close to dropping the boxes containing the china and crystal she'd inherited from her grandmother. Fortunately, she'd packed each box with enough bubble wrap to protect the treasures of King Tut's tomb. The movers wouldn't let her ride in the truck with them — "insurance reasons," the guy said — so she had to take a cab to the new apartment. Andrew Weisch had notified the doorman that the new resident of 18D would be moving on the morning of the first, so the freight elevator was ready when she arrived.

The movers carried her bed and her chest of drawers to the master bedroom and her computer desk and PC to the second bedroom. They left everything else in a pile on the living room floor. Her old place had been jam-packed from floor to ceiling. Now, in 18D, she realized how little she owned.

The movers gone, she popped open a Diet Coke and threw herself onto the couch, which the movers had positioned to allow for the best view of Central Park. The feeling was indescribable, Corinne thought. This was the moment that every Manhattanite longs for — the minute she moves into the apartment of her dreams.

Her cell phone beeped — new voice message. She punched in her password and heard a chipper greeting from her best friend Jeanine Habel, inviting herself over to see the new place. She'd dialed half of Jeanine's number when she heard a doorknob jiggle. She turned her head toward the front door of the apartment and watched it swing open. Into the room walked a funky looking East Village type with dark sunglasses, messy blond hair, and dirty jeans. He looked about Corinne's age, 35 or 36. He was carrying a box and seemed preoccupied. Then he looked up and saw her lying on the couch.

"Hi," he said, somewhat coldly. "Sorry, I thought you'd be gone by now."

"Excuse me?"

"Listen, I'm paying for the truck by the hour. Would you mind if we just put my stuff to one side while you wait for your guys to get here?"

"I think there must be a mistake, Mr. . . . ?"

"Ian. What kind of mistake?"

"I'm not moving out. I just moved *in*."

"Huh?"

Ian and Corinne stared at each other, confused.

They were searching for the right words when a stunning black woman in her early thirties popped her head in the door.

"Hello," she said, smiling. She looked at the boxes strewn across the living room floor. "Are you the former tenants?"

"No, we're the new tenants," Corinne said. "I mean, we both think we're the new tenants."

"I don't understand," the woman said.

"Neither do we," said Ian.

Corinne bit her lip. "Something funny's going on."

There was a knock at the open door. The shaved head of a man in his late twenties peeked into the apartment.

"Hey, what's up?" asked the newcomer.

"Hello," said Corinne and Ian, simultaneously.

"I'm gonna start bringing my stuff up now, if that's OK."

Corinne, Ian, and the unnamed woman looked at one another, then at the new guy.

"Looks like we have a problem," Corinne said.

3

The four new tenants sat on various couches in the living room trying to make sense of their predicament. They'd spent the last two hours on their cell phones in search of answers. By exchanging tales of how they'd come to Apartment 18D and what they'd learned from various sources, they were able to piece most of the story together.

Much of the information they'd been given by Andrew Weisch turned out to be true. The apartment was indeed owned by Mr. John Blackmore, a pharmaceuticals magnate who owned apartments in New York, San Francisco, London, Palm Springs, Paris, Frankfurt, Singapore, Johannesburg, and Sydney. Blackmore had recently purchased a larger, even more luxurious apartment in Manhattan, but he was reluctant to give 18D up. He had a teenage daughter at his estate in Mountain View, California, and she was seriously considering attending either Columbia or NYU two years hence. He wanted Apartment 18D to be available if she needed it. Given the upward spiral of Manhattan real estate prices, it made sense for him to hold onto 18D and rent it for a few years instead of selling it now and buying something new if and when the young lady came East. In the meantime, Mr. Blackmore had moved into his new penthouse in SoHo. Corinne learned all this from Mr. Blackmore's new personal assistant.

Mr. Blackmore's former assistant, the nefarious Andrew Weisch, apparently held a grudge against his longtime employer. He'd nursed this grudge secretly for years, the new assistant said. Weisch had left their employ a few weeks ago, and each day they discovered new trouble that he'd carefully plotted. He'd written a letter in Mr. Blackmore's name to the Museum of Modern Art, calling the board of directors a bunch of "bleeding heart liberal freaks" and cutting off the millions that he donated each year. He'd donated Mr. Blackmore's Sydney apartment to a nonprofit hospice that was now housing sixteen terminally ill patients there. He'd even sold Mr. Blackmore's Lamborghini to a New Jersey teenager who'd paid only $3,000 for it.

tment
three,
rental
er she'd
ture was

ht about
ore can't
provided
I hope it

," said Ol-
sure some
around a

Venice said
many times
catch-all cat-

curtly. "There
re, but they're
or ambulance
.A. One of the
nan what cafete-
do you think I
badly? My old
nscale, to put it
me for now that
d, which it seems

taken the opportunity to
during his mischievous
accountants had dis-
425,000 missing from
accounts. Each indi-
been so tiny as not
otice. In addition to
d from each of the
Veisch had kept the
ini, as well as the
old Mrs. Black-
anniversary ring

it seemed, had
ge of renting
supposed to
at $15,000

anything
ding the
said as
n while
Weisch
akes it
stuff
the
wh
r

had been closely reading the apar
lease she'd signed. Like the other
she'd received the countersigned
agreement via FedEx a few days aft
met with Weisch. Blackmore's signa
scribbled above her own.

"Hmmm," she said. "You're rig
the way the lease is written. Blackn
throw us out for at least two years
this is really his signature, which
is."

"But this place is a *penthouse*
iver, of the shaved head. "I'm
dirtbag lawyer can find a wa
couple of signatures."

"Uh, we're not all dirtbags,"
in a tone that conveyed how
she'd been lumped into that
egory.

"Oh. Sorry, dude."

"It's all right," Venice said
are a lot of dirtbags out the
usually in criminal defense
chasing. I'm an Assistant D
good guys working for less t
ria workers make. Why
vanted this apartment so
ace on Avenue C is dov
ldly. Anyway, let's assu
lease is good and soli

to be. That means that whoever gets this place, gets to live here for the two full years at six hundred bucks a month."

"You have to give Weisch a certain amount of credit," Corinne said bitterly. "He really covered all his bases. I talked to the doorman. The morning guy leaves at two p.m., which is when the afternoon guy arrives. So Weisch said that Ian and I were new roommates, and he said the same thing about Venice and Oliver. He scheduled me and Ian to move in during the morning doorman's shift, and Oliver and Venice to move in during the afternoon doorman's shift. That way, no one would get suspicious about four separate people all trying to move into the same apartment, with four different sets of furniture and four different moving companies."

■ ■ ■ ■

A Game of Chance

■ ■ ■ ■

1

They all looked around the apartment at their various piles of stuff, which they'd had no choice but to move in.

Corinne sighed and continued.

"Well, I guess the good news is, one of us gets to keep the apartment. But which one?"

"We should find a way to decide this sooner rather than later," Venice said. "I would love to stay here as much as any of you. But if I work fast, I can probably get my old apartment back." Then she added, "Or, if I get to keep this place, I could get my old place back and let one of you have it. It's far from glamorous, but it's affordable."

"It's got to be better than the place I moved out of," Ian said. "And the East Village is a much better place for an artist than Washington Heights. But I'd rather stay here."

"This stinks," Oliver said. "First my dog

dies, then I break up with my girlfriend, now this."

"I have an idea," Corinne said, matter-of-factly. "Do we all agree that only one of us can stay?"

Everyone in the room nodded.

Corinne began rummaging through the boxes on the living room floor. A minute later she returned with the Yahtzee game she'd owned for decades. She explained her brainstorm.

"There are five dice in here. We each roll all five dice three times. Whoever gets the highest combined score gets to keep the apartment. If there are any ties, the people who are tied roll three more times until the tie is broken."

The four highly disappointed, recently ripped-off people looked at one another.

"Well, at least it gives all of us an equal chance," Venice said. "Sounds like as good a system as any."

"I agree," Ian said.

"What the heck. Let's get it over with," Oliver said.

"OK, should we do it alphabetically?"
Everyone nodded.

Corinne rolled first — 24, 22, and 17.
Ian rolled second — 12, 16, and 21.
Oliver threw 8, 14, and 11.

Venice's three rolls were 17, 16, and 20.

Venice shook Corinne's hand. "Congratulations. Best of luck in your new home. Now let me get on the horn with my greedy landlord before he lets some drug dealers move into my place."

2

Corinne lived very happily in the apartment for two years. The first year, she spent a lot of time at home on the couch, reading the *New York Times* and admiring the view. The second year, she met Javier, a friend whom Jeanine brought to one of Corinne's monthly cocktail parties. They married two months before the lease was up. Using their combined savings, they bought a small home in Dobbs Ferry, New York, and raised two children there.

Venice was able to move back into her old digs on Avenue C, though she ended up spending $200 more per month for the same apartment. She successfully prosecuted several high-profile cases, then was offered a high-paying political position in the mayor's office. She bought a comfortable two-bedroom place in Greenwich Village near Washington Square, where she still lives.

Ian crashed with an artist friend in a loft in the meat packing district until he could find another apartment. An art dealer stopped by the loft to take a look at the friend's work, and she hated it. But she loved Ian's. He had his first show three months later, and 22 of the 25 exhibited pieces sold at good prices. Ian gave half the money to the struggling friend who'd helped him get discovered and used the other half to move into a TriBeCa loft with ample workspace.

Oliver moved in with his parents, who weren't overjoyed at having their peaceful empty nest invaded. Two weeks after he moved back, he came home to find that his mother had fallen down the basement steps. Doctors said that if Oliver hadn't discovered her when he did, she would have died. The Pappas family agreed that Oliver's loss of Apartment 18D was the best thing that ever happened to them.

■ ■ ■ ■

EVERY MAN FOR
HIMSELF

■ ■ ■ ■

1

They all looked around the apartment at
their various piles of stuff, which they'd had
no choice but to move in.

Corinne sighed and continued.

"Well, I guess the good news is, one of us
gets to keep the apartment. But which one?"

They were all physically exhausted from
moving and emotionally drained by the
day's events, so they decided to accept their
fate as the most temporary of roommates.
They spent the night sprawled out on their
various mattresses in various rooms of the
apartment, then reconvened the next morning.

Corinne surveyed the room. *Only in Manhattan could something like this happen,* she
thought.

"I thought about this all night," Venice
began, breaking the ice. "I'm sure we all
considered calling our lawyers and having
them fight it out, but that's not going to

work. The way the contract's written, none of us has more of a right to be here than the other three. In fact, not only would getting lawyers involved not work, it might also backfire, because then Blackmore's attorneys would jump in, and then *none* of us would end up getting to stay. So can we agree that calling our lawyers isn't the way to go?"

They all agreed.

"So, we have to come up with some other way to figure out who gets the apartment," Venice continued. "Any ideas?"

Corinne raised her hand, as if she were still in grammar school. "I was thinking that maybe we could each tell something about ourselves and why we feel we deserve the apartment. Then we could take a vote, and whoever wins gets to stay."

They all agreed that it was worth a try. Corinne went first.

"I'm Corinne Jensen. I'm originally from Buffalo. I moved here after college twelve years ago. I'm a book editor. I work long hours and make no money. I swear to God — I'll show you copies of my tax returns. I brown-bag it to work every day, and I have zero savings. I got thrown out of my last apartment because it was going co-op and I couldn't afford the down payment. I was going to stash away every dime I saved from living here so that I could buy myself a small place when the lease is up. Then at least I wouldn't spend the rest of my life at the mercy of some greedy landlord."

It was Ian's turn. "I'm Ian McTeague. My last place was a roach-infested studio in Washington Heights, which I moved into because it was the only place I could afford. In the two years I lived there, I got mugged three times. To pay the rent I do freelance design. Corporate logos, matchbook covers, anything. But I'm really in the City to be an artist. And I can't schmooze the art community from a smelly studio on a block full of crack dealers. I need a place where I can work without worrying that I'm going to be murdered. Most of all, I need this apartment to display my work and throw parties. It's the only way I'll get anywhere. You have no idea what it takes to be an artist in this city."

Venice spoke. "You all know I'm Venice. Pronounced 'Ven-eece,' spelled like the town in Italy. My last name is Calderon. I'm African-American on my mother's side and Latina on my father's side. I grew up in Maspeth, Queens. My parents never made more than $40,000 a year between them their entire lives, but they spent $80,000 to send me to college and another $80,000 to send me to law school. I work for the Manhattan D.A.'s office, where I prosecute perverts and sickos who would love nothing more than to kill you for the change in your pocket. I don't want to sound like a martyr, but I could make a lot more money being a defense lawyer. *A lot* more money. I'm a D.A. because it's what I believe in. Why do I deserve this apartment? Because without people like me, people like you guys wouldn't dare to live in this city. D.A.'s get no perks. None. But we do get paid next to nothing for doing a job that could get us killed. I'm not saying the three of you don't deserve this place, but I think I do, too."

There was a quiet moment, then Oliver began speaking. "I'm Oliver Pappas. I grew up here on the Upper West Side. My folks still live in their house on 93rd Street with my crabby grandmother. My father is a total jerk and my mother is his slave, so there's no way I'll ever move back there. I work with computers. I make an OK living but I'm not getting rich. I've always had room-mates and I was psyched to finally get a place to myself. Girls don't like to date guys who don't have their own places, in case you didn't know. So maybe I'm not an editor or an artist or a lawyer, but I'm cool and nice and that's it. Plus I gave my last three grand to Andrew Weisch."

After a moment, Corinne said, "OK. Good. Now let's get this over with." She handed a piece of paper and a pencil to each person in the room. "Just write down who you think should get the apartment. Then drop your ballot in this vase. Whoever gets the most votes gets to stay. We all agree to that, right?"

Everyone murmured yes. Corinne could feel her heart beating practically out of her chest.

The four contenders went into separate rooms to write down their votes. A minute later, all the votes were in the vase.

"Corinne, it was your idea," Venice said. "Why don't you read the votes?"

Corinne picked up the vase. One by one, she read from each slip of paper.

"Venice. . . . Oliver. . . . Corinne. . . . Ian." She sighed. "Well, I guess we're back to square one."

2

They all agreed that they needed more time to think. So they decided to meet again at the end of the day to brainstorm more possibilities. By seven p.m., they were once again seated in a circle, sipping coffee and noshing on munchies that Corinne had picked up at Zabar's.

They spent the next three hours considering and rejecting various ideas, all of which seemed to favor the suggester over the others.

Around ten o'clock, Oliver had an idea. "Maybe we should have a contest. You know, a competition or something."

"Hmmm," Venice said. "That's an interesting idea."

"How about this?" Ollie suggested. "Each of us writes down a contest on a piece of paper. We put the papers into the vase and choose one. That becomes the contest."

"I'm willing to try that," Corinne said,

"but only if the contest doesn't give anyone an unfair advantage. For example, it couldn't be something like who can lift the heaviest weights, or who owns the most lipstick."

Venice spoke up. "How about this? We pick a slip of paper from the vase. Then at least three of us have to agree that it's fair. If at least three don't agree, we choose the next slip of paper and vote again. And we keep coming up with contest ideas until one wins."

"I'd go for that," Corinne said.

"Sounds all right to me," agreed Ian.

"I'm in," said Oliver.

"It's unanimous, then," Venice said. "Let's take half an hour to come up with our contests, then meet back here."

They separated. Thirty-five minutes later, Ian reached into the vase and pulled out a slip of paper. He unfolded the paper and read:

The person who stays in the apartment the longest gets to keep it.

If someone leaves the apartment for any reason, that person cannot keep the apartment. That person must then leave the apartment immediately, accepting his or her fate with no complaints. The contest begins now.

"Let's vote," Ian said. "All in favor, raise your hand."

Everyone raised a hand except Venice.

Corinne looked at her three roommates. "Looks like we have a winner."

"We should all sign an agreement that the apartment goes to the winner of this contest," Venice suggested. "Just to be on the safe side."

So they did.

3

To determine who would live where, they wrote their names and the apartment's rooms on individual slips of paper. All the occupants went into one vase, all the rooms into another. To match the person with the room, they chose one slip from Jar A and one slip from Jar B. Venice got the master bedroom. Ian got the second bedroom. Corinne got the living room, and Oliver ended up with the dining room. Venice had exclusive use of the master bath, and the other three could use the two bathrooms on the first and second floors. The rooms thus assigned, the four roommates spent the next day setting up their spaces for what looked to be a long, drawn-out competition.

Corinne had a good relationship with her editor-in-chief, Martin Donovan. After Corinne explained the situation, he agreed to allow Corinne to work from home for two weeks. Thanks to the many phone jacks and Internet ports throughout Apartment 18D, it was easy for Corinne to set up a mini-workstation in her living room/bedroom combination.

Ian set up a mini-studio in his bedroom; one benefit of being an artist was his ability to work anywhere he had his Mac, his canvases, and his acrylics. Oliver had a couple of weeks of banked sick time and decided to take it one day at a time, calling in sick each morning until he couldn't get away with it any more. He knew he'd get fired eventually, but it would be easier to find another job than it would be to find another apartment like 18D.

Venice had it the worst. Her job required her to be in her office or in court all day. She managed to buy a few days by telling her supervisor that she'd sprained her ankle and was likely to be apartment-bound for at least a week. For an added touch of realism, she closed the conversation by saying, "You'd better send me the short-term disability paperwork, just in case."

Corinne's assistant arrived every few days with a satchelful of work. Venice got daily deliveries from FedEx or UPS. And occasionally a colleague from the D.A.'s office stopped by to drop off or pick up documents.

4

They all wanted the apartment. They all wanted it badly.

But they weren't unethical or evil people.

They were going to abide by the rules.

There was no animosity. They were sure they'd remain on cordial terms even after the winner had been declared.

Who knew how long they'd be together in Apartment 18D? Getting along was in their best interests.

There would be no hard feelings when the contest was over.

May the best person win.

5

Meals were brought in every few hours and paid for by credit card. Sometimes two or three of the new roommates would eat breakfast, lunch, or dinner together; sometimes they'd dine alone. Everyone had a cell phone, which kept all of them in contact with the outside world. Venice and Ian could retire to their bedrooms when they wanted privacy. If Corinne or Oliver wanted to talk on the phone in private, they'd sit in one of the bathrooms.

On their fourth night in the apartment, Corinne, Oliver, and Venice sat around the kitchen table, eating pizza and drinking Jack Daniel's and Coke. As more JD was consumed, the conversation turned to relationships, and Corinne found herself talking about her most recent romantic fiasco. After taking her out on five lovely dates, Ezra had simply stopped calling her. She'd spent the last few weeks trying to figure out why.

"You could have called him, you know," Oliver said.

"You're better off without him," Venice said, refusing to get riled up by the general jerkiness of men.

"Relationships are a pain," Oliver opined. "I just broke up with my girlfriend, and it was totally the best move I ever made. She always wanted to party. I mean, a little on the weekends is fine, but she wanted to do it all the time. Then she'd get all weird on me." He shrugged his shoulders.

"When you say 'party,' do you mean drink? Or do drugs?" Corinne asked, pouring them their fourth Jack and Coke.

"Both, I guess," Ollie replied. "But nothing heavy. Just once in a while. You know. That's why we broke up."

"You should trade tips with Ian," Corinne suggested. "I've smelled some interesting scents wafting out from under his bedroom door."

"Why doesn't Ian ever hang out with us? We're cool and fun." Oliver sounded hurt.

"Who knows?" Venice said in a tone that also implied *And who cares?* "Let him do what he wants up there in his bedroom. No skin off our backs."

"I'm wondering: If Ian had to choose, would he pick a girlfriend or a boyfriend?"

Oliver asked.

"Boyfriend," Venice decreed, with great confidence.

"Agreed," said Corinne. "Why are the nice looking ones always gay?"

"Someone has the hots for Ian," Oliver said in a singsong voice.

"No way," Corinne protested, giggling, which was tantamount to admitting the exact opposite.

"What about you, Ven? You dating anybody?" Oliver asked. He called Venice "Ven," Corinne "Cor," and Ian "E."

Venice waved a hand. "Nobody worth mentioning."

"Come on, Ven, you're among friends."

"There's really nothing to talk about."

"No cute prosecutors at the courthouse?" Corinne asked. "Or how about those lawyers fresh out of law school, with their nice suits and new shoes? Some of them are pretty handsome, I have to admit. Young JFK, Jr. types."

"I find most of them rather boring."

"One of the guys I went to high school with is a D.A. downtown," Oliver said. "Jerry Miceli. You know him?"

"I think I've heard the name, but there's a lot of us," Venice said, evasively.

"I think he works on Court Street, hangs

out at the Union Pub on Maiden Lane . . . Says it's a big hangout for the D.A.'s or prosecutors or whatever you call them. I hung out there with him once and none of the girls would even look at me. Guess I don't look like a lawyer, huh? No yuppie haircut. Well, no hair, period. You ever go there?"

"Once in a while."

"You ever try that stupid bucking bronco in the pool room? Jerry almost broke his neck on it."

"Not my cup of tea."

"Ever date anyone you met there? It's a total singles scene, according to Jerry."

"I'm going to bed," Venice said, and stumbled up the stairs to her bedroom.

"Boy, she's uptight," Oliver pouted.

"She's just drunk, like us. I'm going to bed, too." Corinne stood up and tried to clear the paper plates and close the pizza boxes. Instead she spilled her drink, dropped the paper plates, and knocked the pizza boxes onto the floor.

Oliver attempted to stand up, too. "We'll clean up in the morning. Come on, I'll help you get to your bed. But then who's gonna help me? Well, I'll figure it out, I guess."

They stumbled to Corinne's bed, arms wrapped around each other's waists and shoulders. Oliver gave Corinne a slight push and she tumbled onto her bed. She was asleep instantly. Oliver looked across the living room to where his twin bed sat against the dining room wall 50 feet away. The distance seemed much, much greater.

"It's not gonna happen," he said to no one, grabbing a pillow from Corinne's bed and throwing it to the hardwood floor. In sixty seconds he was snoring as peacefully as Corinne.

6

They were wakened the next morning by the sound of Ian freaking out.

"What! What is this? What's *wrong* with you people?"

Corinne hauled herself out of bed and nearly stepped on Oliver. Her head hurt.

"What's the matter? Ian, what is it?"

Ian was in the kitchen, running hot water and dumping a bottle of Clorox bleach into a plastic bucket. He reached into one of the boxes piled on the kitchen floor and pulled out a pair of new rubber dishwashing gloves.

"Look at this food all over the floor! Don't you know this is what brings rats and mice and cockroaches?"

Oliver, a bit unsteady on his feet, said, "Calm down, E. It's just a couple of slices of pizza."

Ian had fashioned a sort of makeshift bandana out of a clean dish towel and wrapped it around his head. He was on his knees scrubbing, scrubbing, scrubbing like a madman.

Venice, slightly wobbly, came down the stairs and joined them in the kitchen.

"Ian, you look ridiculous," she said, laughing.

"Stop laughing," Ian said through clenched teeth. "You people want rats and mice and roaches infesting this place? They all carry disease! Disease!"

Corinne, Oliver, and Venice looked at one another, and said nothing more.

7

Oliver thought, *I don't like that woman, and I don't trust her. Not for one second.*

He didn't like the way she condescended to him, the way she thought she was smarter than everyone else. Everyone always thought they were smarter than Oliver, but he'd proven people wrong in the past, and he planned on doing so again. Of course, that meant playing dumb for as long as it took to get the apartment.

He'd been suspicious of Venice from the minute he met her. He could smell a phony a mile away, and she reeked of phoniness.

That was why he'd asked her about the Union Pub on Maiden Lane. There was no Union Pub on Maiden Lane. And he didn't have a friend named Jerry Miceli. Therefore, Venice couldn't have "heard the name" Jerry Miceli, and she couldn't have seen the nonexistent bucking bronco in the nonexistent Union Pub.

If she'd lied about that, what else was she lying about?

8

Locked in her bedroom and standing as far from the door as possible, Venice was speaking softly into her cell phone.

"Warren, you've got to move more quickly on this. These people are as determined as I am. Did you do what I asked?"

She listened a moment.

"Darn. I figured it was a long shot. OK, here's the new plan. You know some of the senior partners at Callen and Dixon, right? They represent Blackmore. Call in some favors. Get them to have Blackmore agree that whoever's lease he signed first gets the apartment. His opinion should count for something."

She listened another moment. "No, that's not going to work. . . . The other woman was the first one here. . . . Yes, she can prove it. No, I'm telling you, the dates on the leases are the best way to do it. I saw two of them, and Blackmore signed mine the day before he signed those. . . . Who knows? Maybe Weisch thought Blackmore would get suspicious if he had him signing too many things in one day . . . No, I haven't seen the third one yet. But I'll find it. And if Blackmore signed it before he signed mine, it'll just 'disappear.' "

There was a knock at the door.

"I have to go. Call me as soon as you hear something. I talked them all out of calling their attorneys, but I don't know how long that'll last."

9

Venice quickly sat at her desk and opened a legal manual.

"Come in," she said, calmly.

Corinne entered. "Hey, Venice. Sorry to bother you. I was wondering if I could ask you a favor?"

"Sure."

"No doubt you've noticed that I look horrible."

"Well, I wasn't going to say anything. . . ."

"I'm hung over and I feel gross. Would you mind if I took a hot bath in your bathroom? It has the only bathtub in the apartment. I think it would really help."

Venice smiled. "Go right ahead, Corinne. I was feeling a little woozy myself this morning."

Corinne squealed with delight. Five minutes later she was back, carrying a bathrobe, a change of clothes, a bag of toiletries, a hair dryer, and a cosmetics kit. She walked into the master bath and turned on the spigots. The sound of the water hitting the bathtub hurt her eyeballs but provided excellent camouflage noise as Corinne rifled through Venice's belongings.

The story Venice told wasn't consistent with Corinne's observations. She'd noticed Venice's expensive clothing, jewelry, and accessories as soon as Venice had walked into the apartment. How, Corinne wanted to know, could a woman who struggled to earn a living as an Assistant D.A. afford those two pairs of Manolo Blahnik shoes next to the toilet? Corinne had never seen a pair priced at less than $500, and then only at clearance sales. The robe hanging on the door bore a tag from a members-only prestige retailer on Madison Avenue. And that Prada bag sitting on the vanity wouldn't have cost less than $1400, unless it was counterfeit, which it wasn't.

Venice had to be up to something, and Corinne was going to find out what.

Still, the bath was refreshing. Venice was working at her computer when Corinne emerged from the bathroom.

"Thanks, Venice. I owe you."

10

Was it Oliver's imagination, or did he hear Venice come downstairs in the middle of the night and rifle around in the dining room, as if looking for something? Good thing he'd hidden his rental agreement somewhere safe. She'd seemed a little too interested in it that afternoon.

11

Corinne felt guilty for snooping through Venice's things. So she dug through her boxes and found a box of lovely, expensive soaps she'd received for her birthday. She wrapped them in gift paper and walked upstairs to Venice's room.

She knocked at the door and stuck her head in.

Venice clicked off her cell phone abruptly, swirling around in her chair to block her computer screen.

"Am I bothering you, Venice?"

"You just startled me," Venice replied calmly. "Hold on, let me save my work." She turned to the computer and closed the file she was working on.

Corinne extended her offering. "I just wanted to bring you a little token of thanks. That bath did wonders for me yesterday."

Venice unwrapped the gift. Her eyes widened slightly, very slightly, as she recognized the pricey brand name.

"Corinne, that's sweet of you. But totally unnecessary."

"Well I did appreciate it, Venice."

"I'm sure you would've done the same for me. Oh, Corinne, could I ask you a favor? Could you wait for me to say 'Come in' before you walk in? My folks had a way of barging into my room without knocking when I was a kid, and I've gotten a little neurotic about it." She smiled as if to say, *We all have these little quirks! You'll indulge me, won't you?*

"Absolutely. I'm sorry, Venice. Well, see you at dinner!"

"Would you mind closing the door behind you?"

Corinne did as requested. When the door was firmly shut, she stood in place. A few seconds later she heard Venice's footsteps as she walked over and locked the door from the inside.

12

Corinne was tired of take-out food. She hadn't had a home-cooked meal since moving into Apartment 18D. She took a survey of the inhabitants. A consensus emerged: Everyone would love fresh Mexican food with loads of cilantro and vine-ripened tomatoes. And since they'd be buying tomatoes, why not whip up some gazpacho as well?

Oliver volunteered to help with the cooking, but Corinne adamantly refused. "Thanks, Ollie, but I like my space when I cook. Just sit back and relax. I'm playing chef tonight."

First she prepared the gazpacho, leaving it to cool in a large pot in the refrigerator. Using a ladle, she removed a small amount of the gazpacho and placed it in a separate bowl. Then she cooked and assembled the rest of the food.

Ten minutes before serving the meal, she

visited the first-floor bathroom. She turned on the faucet and gently removed eight Tylenol P.M. sleeping tablets (which she used occasionally) from her pocket. Using the bottom of her electric razor, she crushed the pills into a fine powder. She then wrapped the powder in a piece of toilet paper. Back in the kitchen, she opened the refrigerator and quickly dumped the powder into the large pot of gazpacho.

To ensure that nobody mixed alcohol with the drug, she prepared virgin margaritas and daiquiris. If anyone felt sleepy, they'd attribute it to the nonexistent tequila in the margaritas and the nonexistent rum in the daiquiris. They'd all sleep like babies tonight.

She set the table, then laid out four soup bowls on the kitchen countertop. Checking to make sure nobody was looking, she poured the gazpacho from the small batch into one bowl and the gazpacho from the large batch into the other three bowls.

"Dinner is served," she said to Oliver, who was playing some sort of war game on his computer. Then she hit the intercom buttons to the second-floor bedrooms. "Come on down, guys," she said. "Dinner's ready."

Venice and Ian drained their gazpacho. Venice liked it so much, she had a second bowl. Oliver tasted it and declared, "Yuck. Cold soup. Gonna pass."

Well, two out of three wasn't bad.

13

Oliver watched. Oliver observed.

Ian stayed in his room for hours at a time, emerging only periodically to use the bathroom. He showered three times a day: in the morning, in early afternoon, and at night just before he went to bed, anywhere between ten and midnight. Oliver trusted Ian even less than he trusted Venice.

He knew Venice was up to something. From the two bathrooms he'd spent two days calling the Manhattan D.A.'s offices, only to be told again and again that there was no one named "Venice Calderon" on staff. Which he'd known all along, of course.

Ian had to be up to something, too. What else could he be doing in that room for days at a time? The door was closed most of the time. When it wasn't, Ian could usually be seen scrubbing the hardwood floors or walls with an astringent-smelling cleaning fluid.

After helping Corinne clear the table and

wash the dishes, Venice and Ian both said they felt sleepy and went upstairs. Oliver retired to his dining room/bedroom and turned on his TV set.

He had to time this just right.

A little after 10:00, Corinne went into the bathroom on the first floor — just the opportunity he'd been waiting for. He ran up to the second-floor bathroom and locked himself in.

He'd willingly taken part in many fraternity pranks in college, some of which had been pretty gross. But they paled in comparison to what he was about to do. He unzipped his pants and sat down. After doing his business, he filled the toilet bowl with mounds of toilet paper. Then he flushed and waited for the inevitable cascade.

He ran down the stairs. Corinne was sitting on her bed reading a manuscript.

"Cor! Cor! Do we have a plunger anywhere?"

"You didn't."

"I did."

"How bad is it?"

"Pretty bad. You find a plunger and I'll start cleaning it up." He grabbed a bucket and mop from the kitchen and ran back up the stairs. In the bathroom, he made a lot of noise but didn't do much actual mop-ping.

Corinne came upstairs, averting her nose and eyes from the stink and the mess. "No plunger. I called to have one delivered, but they said they're short-staffed and it's going to take at least an hour."

"This is so embarrassing. Go back down-stairs. I'll take care of everything."

"Gladly," Corinne said, and ran down the stairs as fast as her legs would carry her.

Venice would have no need to use this bathroom; she had one of her own. But Ian wasn't so lucky.

Oliver rapped on Ian's door.

"E, hey listen, the toilet overflowed in the bathroom up here. If you need to go, better use the one downstairs."

Ian wrinkled his face in horror.

"Who's cleaning it up? Who's disinfecting it?"

"I am. Just waiting for a plunger."

"This is unspeakably disgusting. And I was just about to take my shower." Ian shut his bedroom door abruptly.

Ollie returned to the bathroom and waited, paying close attention to Ian's bedroom door as he pretended to mop. There was no way Ian would go into this bathroom tonight, if ever again. Just the way

Oliver wanted it.

A few minutes later, Ian emerged from his room wearing slippers and a robe. He closed the door behind him.

Oliver waited until he heard the water running in the downstairs shower. He stepped into the hallway and closed the bathroom door to give "passersby" the impression that he was still within. In a flash, he was in Ian's room. He figured he had ten minutes.

14

Now was as good a time as any. Corinne peeked her head up the stairs and saw the upstairs bathroom door closed. Ollie must still be in there. Ian was showering in the downstairs bathroom. The coast was as clear as it was going to get.

She hit the intercom button to Venice's room.

"Venice, are you awake?" she asked. No response.

Now!

Corinne sprinted up the stairs to Venice's room and turned the doorknob. It was locked.

She'd expected as much. From her pocket she pulled the keys that Andrew Weisch had given her and unlocked the door, stepping in gingerly.

The Tylenol P.M. had done its job. Venice was snoring quietly after the two bowls of gazpacho. Ian had consumed only one, which meant that he'd gotten close to a normal dose and could probably stay awake for another hour before passing out.

Corinne sat down quietly at Venice's desk. Moonlight shone through the windows and illuminated the desk.

Books on case law, torts, and precedents were everywhere. Corinne picked up one of the books and opened to the first page. There was a stamp on the inside front cover:

**Property of
The Law Offices of Taft, Donohue &
Calderon
New York, NY
DO NOT REMOVE FROM LIBRARY**

Like so many professionals, Venice rarely bothered to turn off her computer. Corinne touched the mouse, and the screen saver quickly reverted to the desktop. The computer had all the standard applications — Microsoft Word, Excel, PowerPoint, and Outlook. She clicked on the Outlook e-mail program. Venice had about 40 saved messages in her inbox and an equal number in her sent items file.

Corinne clicked on one of the sent items. The e-mail was full of legal jargon, but it seemed to be about some sort of corporate merger activity. The signature block read:

Venice J. Calderon, JD, LLD
Senior Partner
Taft, Donohue & Calderon
785 Park Avenue South
New York, New York 10021
212-555-6000, Ext. 317
E-mail: CalderonJ@tdc.com

Half the messages in the inbox were from someone named Deborah Towson. Corinne clicked on one, opening a string of e-mails on which Deborah and Venice had gone back and forth.

>>>Venice,
>>>I can't find those spreadsheets. I'm pretty sure I left them on your chair before you left last Tuesday night. Is it possible you put them somewhere in your office?
>>>Debbie

>>They're not in my office. I have told you at least a dozen times NOT to leave things on my chair. Chairs are for SIT-TING, not for filing papers. I'm NOT going to tell you this again. If you can't find the spreadsheets, you're going to

have to stay late to prepare new ones. NO OVERTIME and NO PAY for this, since it wouldn't have been necessary if you hadn't misplaced them to begin with.

>Venice,
>I'm really sorry. I've looked all over and I can't find them anywhere. I will draft them and bring them to the apartment tomorrow for you to sign.
>Debbie

DO NOT come to the apartment before noon. The time it takes you to get to the apartment from the office is NOT part of your working time. You need to stay late tomorrow night to make up the time.

The signature block on the original message read, "Deborah L. Towson, Administrative Assistant to Venice Calderon, Taft, Donohue & Calderon."

Venice's cell phone was sitting amidst the books and papers. Corinne played with the phone for half a minute, looking for the Call Log menu. When she found it, she took a pencil and sheet of paper from the desk and wrote down the last three incoming phone numbers and the last three outgoing phone numbers. Each phone number had a name attached.

She looked at her watch. She'd been in Venice's room long enough. She tiptoed out, locking the door behind her.

15

This guy truly is a kook, Oliver thought.

In one corner of Ian's room, three large boxes held every cleaning product known to mankind: Mr. Clean, Top Job, Janitor in a Drum, Fantastik, Windex, Clorox, Scrubbing Bubbles. A large laundry bag held dozens of freshly laundered towels.

Oliver hurriedly flipped through two stacks of paper on Ian's drawing table. The first stack included sketches of various abstract designs. The second stack showed elaborate women's clothing designs, highlighted with colored pencils.

Underneath the clothing designs was a small, cheap photo album, the kind sold at Duane Reade drugstores for 99 cents. Oliver flipped through the photos. On every page was a photo of Ian with another man. On the beach, arms around each other's waists. Side by side at some sort of fancy function. On a park bench, a dog between them.

The second guy looked awfully familiar.

Oliver looked at one of the pictures more closely. A puzzle piece clicked into place. The other man was Andrew Weisch.

Oliver looked at his watch. Time to get out of here. He returned the photo album to its original location under the sketches and cautiously opened the bedroom door. As he did, he saw Corinne slip out of Venice's bedroom and slink down the stairs.

He was sitting in the upstairs bathroom sixty seconds later when Ian returned.

Thirty minutes later, the all-night grocery delivered the plunger, and Oliver fixed the mess he'd made.

16

The buzzer buzzed. The doorman announced, "Debbie Towson is here to see you."

Venice was in the kitchen at the time. "Send her up."

Debbie Towson wasn't what Corinne expected. She'd pictured Debbie as a young, slender, well-coiffed mini-Venice in a business suit. Instead, she was a short, slightly overweight middle-aged woman with gray streaks through her black hair.

Venice didn't invite Debbie into the apartment while she rifled through the folders and papers that Debbie had delivered.

"Where are the Huffington materials?" Venice asked angrily.

Debbie looked like a deer caught in a Jeep's headlights. "Did you want them? I've been keeping a list of everything you need, and I know they weren't on there . . ."

"I asked you to bring them when we

talked yesterday."

"I'm sorry, Venice. I don't remember. I'll messenger them to you . . ."

"No," Venice snapped. "Just ask Jude to look them over. And don't leave his office until they're signed. Think you can handle that?"

"I'm sorry, Venice."

"You're always sorry." Venice shut the door without saying "Thank you" or "Good-bye."

Corinne was pouring herself a cup of coffee during the exchange. "Wow, you weren't very nice to her, Venice."

Venice sighed. "I know, I know. I try so hard to be patient, but she's really just incompetent. You have no idea how much extra work she makes for me. I should be putting criminals in prison, and instead I have to track down important files that she lost."

Corinne felt sorry for Debbie, who'd looked as if she'd been beaten with a stick every day of her life.

17

The phone rang. Venice answered, speaking softly. "Hello."

She listened, then said, "No luck. I couldn't find it. I think we have to pursue a different avenue."

She listened again. "It's just as well. I don't want to owe the people at Callen and Dixon any favors, anyway."

18

The cell phone rang. Ian stopped scrubbing the bedroom wall with his homemade ammonia mixture long enough to answer it.

"Hello, this is Ian," he said spacily. He was feeling slightly dizzy from the fumes.

He nearly dropped the phone. "How dare you call me."

He listened a moment.

"I can't believe this, Andrew. Not after what you did to me." He heard his voice getting louder. "No, don't give me that nonsense. Do you have any idea what you got me into? You say we're going to move into this fabulous apartment, so I give up my place . . . and instead you give it to three other people just to get enough money to keep you in coke for a couple of weeks."

Ian was silent for half a minute. "You miss me? You miss me! You've got to be kidding. . . . What? What! You do something like this to me, and you disappear for a month, and

you want me to take you back? Forget it.
. . . Oh, you *would* know if you had to live
with these people . . . Yes, they're still here
. . . Long story, and it's none of your business anyway . . . Why do you think? I have
nowhere else to go. I am completely and utterly ruined, thanks to you. . . .Go ahead,
laugh . . . Right, it's funny. OK, so you got
your revenge . . . Are you happy now? . . .
No, it's not tit for tat . . . This is much
worse. . . . How many times do I have to
tell you, nothing happened! We were together for two years, I didn't do anything
wrong by having dinner with him . . . No,
Andrew. No. I had dinner with an ex-lover,
you left me without a place to live . . . It's
not the same. No. Stop trying to make me
feel bad. OK, yes. Yes. Yes, I guess I miss
you, too . . . I can't believe you would do
this to someone you're supposed to love.
. . . And where are you, anyway? . . ."

Ian laughed. "It's the ultimate revenge,
isn't it? The old creep deserves it for the
way he treated you. . . ."

Ian stopped talking and listened. He
didn't say one word for five minutes.

"Wow, that's really sneaky," he finally said.
"All right, I'll do it. Anything to keep this
place. And the sooner, the better. I'm getting really sick of these freaks."

19

Corinne spent the day enmeshed in research.

Five of the six numbers she'd written down from Venice's call log were direct lines to staff members of Taft, Donohue & Calderon. She'd looked up the company on the Internet and discovered that the firm employed 165 full-time attorneys, specialized in corporate law, and brought in approximately $850 million per year in revenue. Five of the names she'd written down had mini-biographies on the Website's "Staff" section. All of them were partners or senior partners.

She'd also read Venice's Web biography. "Ms. Calderon was born in Los Angeles, California, where she served as Assistant District Attorney from 1993 to 1995. After joining the company's L.A. office in 1996, she moved to the New York City office in 1998. The company changed its name from

Taft & Donohue to Taft, Donohue & Calderon when she became an equity partner in 2001."

Well, at least Venice had told at least one partial truth — she *had* been an Assistant District Attorney, albeit years earlier.

The sixth number belonged to someone named Warren Burgess. Corinne locked herself in the bathroom and dialed the number.

"Mr. Burgess's line."

"Hello," Corinne said. "Is Warren Burgess available?"

"May I ask who's calling?" The voice was professional but suspicious.

"This is Rose Williams. Maybe you can help me? I'd promised to send Warren a check for the money I owe him, but I seem to have misplaced his address. Would you give that to me, please?"

"Of course. Burgess & Burgess, 101 Fifth Avenue, New York, New York 10003."

Corinne logged onto the Internet again and searched for Burgess & Burgess, which turned out to be an even larger firm, with even more prestigious clients, than Taft, Donohue & Calderon. Warren Burgess was the top gun.

So much for not getting lawyers involved.

20

She'd stopped asking him to look at his lease. Why?

He'd take care of her. He had a plan. But first, there was Ian to attend to. He had to be in cahoots with Weisch, didn't he?

That was the order he'd get rid of them: First Ian, then Venice, then Corinne. He liked Corinne the most, but she had to be up to no good. Why else would she have sneaked into Venice's bedroom while she was asleep?

21

Venice placed a call to Warren first thing in the morning.

"Are your sons in town?" she asked.

She listened for a second. "OK. Good. Have you talked to Herrold yet? Great. Here's what we're going to do. . . ."

22

"Ollie, you eating with us tonight?" Corinne asked. "I was thinking maybe Thai food."

Oliver didn't get up from his bed, on which he'd been lying all day.

Corinne moved closer. "Ollie."

No response.

"Ollie?"

No response.

She touched his shoulder. "Ollie, are you OK?"

Oliver's eyes opened slightly. "Uhhhhhh," he groaned. "I feel awful."

"What's wrong?"

"I don't know, I've been feeling sick ever since that episode in the bathroom." He clutched his stomach and groaned.

"Can I get you anything? Pepto Bismol? Mylanta?"

Oliver tried to raise himself onto his arm but fell back onto the bed. "Yeah . . . ow . . . I haven't felt this bad since I had food poisoning."

Corinne retrieved the Pepto and poured the pink liquid into a tablespoon. She held it to Oliver's mouth as he struggled to hold his head up.

"Ollie, you look really bad. Maybe I should call a doctor. What if it *is* food poisoning?" Could her inexpert Mexican cooking-cum-Tylenol P.M. have caused this much gastric distress?

"No, I'll be all right." The last few words slurred as Ollie dropped off to sleep.

The thought of food poisoning scared Corinne enough to prevent her from calling the Thai place. Instead, she had the deli deliver a green salad, which she washed thoroughly for about fifteen minutes. Venice and Ian could fend for themselves for dinner.

23

The next morning, Corinne woke early and checked on Oliver. He'd been tossing and turning all night, and the bedclothes were in a state of disarray.

Venice and Ian had ordered dinner on their own the evening before, and both had come downstairs only long enough to pay the delivery people. Neither, it seemed, wanted much to do with poor, sick Ollie, especially Ian. And neither came downstairs in the morning to see how he was doing.

Ollie seemed basically unconscious, but Corinne still didn't feel safe talking on the phone with him sleeping so near. So she took her cell phone into the bathroom and dialed the number. She'd rehearsed what she would say. One of two things could happen. Either it would work beautifully, or it would backfire and things would get ugly.

The phone picked up on the second ring.

"Good morning," Corinne said. "I have a

proposition for you."

"Who is this?"

"Do you like Venice Calderon?"

Silence.

"What would you say if I told you we can work together to teach Venice a valuable lesson?"

Two seconds of silence. Then, "Who *is* this? Tell me, or I'm hanging up."

"Please don't hang up. Just hear me out. You'll like my idea."

More silence. Then: "I'm listening."

24

Noon came, and Oliver was still tossing, turning, and shivering.

Corinne got some cold water and wiped down his forehead. Then she shook him gently until he swam into consciousness.

"Ollie. Ollie. I want to call a doctor for you. You're not getting any better."

Oliver moaned in pain. "OK. OK. It's Dr. Marino. Look in my book . . . it's on the desk. . . ."

Corinne rifled through the mess on the desk and found a phone book stuffed with papers, scraps, and business cards. She turned to M and found Dr. Marino's number, then used her cell to call the doctor's office.

"Doctor's office," said a receptionisty voice.

"Hello, this is Corinne Jensen calling. A friend of mine, Oliver Pappas, is a patient of yours, I believe."

"Let me pull the record . . . how do you spell the last name?"

"P-a-p-p-a-s."

"Yes, here it is. How can I help you?"

"He's really sick. We think it's food poisoning. He can barely move, he hasn't been out of bed in two days."

"2:30?"

Corinne turned to Oliver. "They can see you at 2:30. We have to find a way to get you there."

"No," Oliver said, though he was doubled over in pain. "Tell him he has to come here. I'm not leaving."

"Oliver, you're sick, you need to see a doctor."

"Forget it."

Corinne turned back to the phone. "Miss, he's . . . uh . . . he's unable to move. We live on a high floor and he wouldn't make it out of the building. Can you send someone here? We're on 72nd at Central Park West."

"Hold, please." The receptionist returned a few minutes later. "We work with an emergency service that makes house calls. Dr. Zahariades can see Mr. Pappas at 3 p.m. And please let Mr. Pappas know that his co-pay on in-home calls is 50% of the doctor's fee."

"I'll tell him," Corinne said, biting back a

sarcastic comment. She gave the receptionist the address and hung up.

25

Dr. Zahariades arrived just before 3:00. He was a short man in his mid-fifties with a white beard and messy white hair. Corinne brought him to Ollie's bed and moved her work into the kitchen to give doctor and patient some privacy.

Ten minutes later Corinne looked up and saw the doctor standing in the doorway. "Excuse me, Miss. . . ."

"Jensen. Corinne Jensen."

"Miss Jensen, are you caring for Mr. Pappas?"

"Well, I guess I am."

"I don't want to alarm you, but he has all the symptoms of a serious strain of botulism that's going around. I've taken a blood sample, which I'm going to have analyzed this afternoon. If it comes back positive, he'll have to be admitted to the hospital."

"Did you tell him that?"

"Yes, but he's fighting me. Miss Jensen,

people have been known to die from this particular strain of *E. coli.* It's very serious."

"Doctor, I don't know what to do. . . ."

"Give me your phone number, and I'll call you when the lab results are in. In the meantime, don't panic. But don't get too close to him, just in case."

Corinne gulped.

26

When the cell phone rang at 7:47 p.m., Corinne nearly jumped out of her skin. She pushed the "Talk" button with trembling fingers.

"Hello?"

"Miss Jensen? This is Dr. Zahariades."

"Is Ollie OK?"

"Mr. Pappas doesn't have botulism. He has a tropical virus called expurgitis. It's rare in this country, but common in undeveloped nations where people come into contact with untreated fecal matter."

Corinne remembered the toilet clogging incident from a few days earlier. Could it have led to this?

The doctor continued. "The good news is that expurgitis can be treated, but the recovery time is at least two or three months. The bad news is, expurgitis is highly contagious. Mr. Pappas needs to be quarantined until I find a hospital to admit him. Until then, you and your roommates should avoid all contact with him. Please don't leave the apartment. I'll stop by at nine tomorrow morning to take blood samples from all of you."

She had to tell the others. And, perhaps more importantly, she had to get away from Ollie.

She ran up the stairs and banged first on Venice's door, then on Ian's. They answered simultaneously, Ian looking dazed and Venice looking irritated. Both sensed her urgency.

"What's wrong?" Venice asked.

"The doctor just called with Ollie's lab results. He has a tropical virus called expurgitis. It's highly contagious and Ollie has to be quarantined until they come to take him to the hospital. . . ."

She didn't finish her sentence. Ian started to scream and bang his fist against the wall. He ran in a circle like a caged animal. His screams got louder and louder.

Fifteen seconds later, Venice and Corinne heard the front door slam behind Ian as he ran out of the apartment as fast as his legs would carry him.

27

That left just the three of them. Corinne assumed that Ian would be back to get his stuff at some point, but until then, his room was free, and that's where she planned to stay. She went downstairs, grabbed a few personal items, and returned to the second bedroom. She wasn't going anywhere near Oliver, ever again.

Back in her room, Venice had logged onto WebMD and the Website of the American Medical Association. Nowhere on the Web was expurgitis listed as a disease. In fact, it wasn't even a word.

Kudos, Oliver, she thought. *You're smarter than you look.*

28

Downstairs, Oliver slept peacefully. Tossing and turning all night, two nights in a row, had been a lot of work, and he was tired.

He smiled. His uncle, a union electrician, had been quite convincing as Dr. Zahariades. And his friend Cypress, a struggling actress from the neighborhood, had done a bang-up job as the briskly officious receptionist.

29

At 7:30 a.m., they were awakened by a loud banging on the apartment door. Could it be the people from the sanitarium, or wherever Ollie was about to be shipped off to?

Corinne threw on her bathrobe and answered the door. Venice came downstairs to investigate the commotion. Through the peephole Corinne saw two burly policemen. She opened the door.

"We're looking for Oliver Pappas. Is he here?"

"Yes . . . but he's very sick."

"We need to come in, Ma'am," the first officer said. He looked like Hulk Hogan.

The officers entered. The second policeman, who looked like Jesse Ventura, found Ollie lying in bed.

"Oliver Pappas?"

Oliver looked up weakly. "Yeah?"

"You're under arrest for trafficking in illegal substances." He pulled Ollie out of bed in one strong motion and slapped a pair of handcuffs on him. "You have the right to remain silent. You have the right to an attorney. . . ."

"Hey! What is this? What's going on?" Oliver suddenly seemed much stronger.

"We know what you've been up to, Mr. Pappas. Selling drugs in a school zone, for starters."

"What? No way."

"You don't wanna go making your ex-girlfriends mad," the first cop said. "When they get caught, the first thing they do is rat out the guys who get them their drugs."

"What? I never sold anything, I swear, never. . . ."

"Tell it to the judge," the second cop said. "Out you go." He gave Oliver a shove on the back, pushing him toward the front door.

"You shouldn't be touching him," Corinne said. "He has a contagious disease."

"Good one, lady," Jesse Ventura said. "Haven't heard that one before."

The door closed behind them.

Looked like it was down to just her and Venice.

30

"I always thought there was something shady about him," Venice said as she walked up the stairs. Once inside her bedroom, she picked up the phone and dialed. Voice mail picked up.

"Warren? It worked. Tell your sons to send me the bills for the costume rentals."

She clicked the phone off. All she needed was one more day.

Expurgitis. Oh, please.

31

Corinne's phone rang at 8:30.

"Miss Jensen? Dr. Zahariades. I have good news. There's been a mistake."

"A mistake?"

"The lab gave me the wrong test results. Mr. Pappas does *not* have expurgitis. It's just a simple stomach flu. He'll be fine in a day or two."

"You mean there's no tropical illness and no contagion?"

"That's correct. I'm so sorry if I alarmed you. Is Mr. Pappas awake? I'd like to speak with him."

"He's not here, Doctor."

"Not there?"

"No, he's been arrested."

"Arrested?"

32

The buzzer rang at noon. Corinne was sitting in the kitchen eating a light lunch. Venice was in her bedroom.

"Debbie Towson is on her way up," the doorman said.

Corinne hit the intercom to Venice's room. "Debbie Towson is on her way up."

"What's *she* doing here?" Venice asked, sounding angry.

Debbie entered the apartment a minute later, looking as beaten down as ever.

"Venice," Debbie started tentatively. "Sorry to surprise you like this, but I tried to reach you on your cell, and I kept getting knocked straight into voice mail."

"What is it?"

"Mr. Burgess asked me to bring you this." She handed Venice a medium-sized brown accordion folder. "He has to go to court this morning, but he said you'd want these documents right away."

Venice sliced open the sealing tape on the accordion folder and pulled out several pieces of paper.

She smiled as she read the first page, and kept smiling as she read the second, third, and fourth pages.

Venice handed the sheaf of papers to Corinne. "Sorry, Corinne."

Corinne reached out and took the papers. The first sheet was a piece of expensive letterhead embossed with "Burgess & Burgess." The note was brief:

Venice,
The documents are enclosed. The apartment is yours. Judge Herrold made the judgment this morning. I've asked Debbie to hand deliver this to you because I've been unable to reach you on your cell phone.

Let's celebrate. Meet me for lunch at 12:30 at Tavern on the Green. My treat.
Yours,
Warren

The second, third, and fourth pages were stapled together. The details of the case were summarized and a judgment was entered: Exclusive occupancy of Apartment 18D at 8 West 72nd Street was granted to

Venice Calderon.

Corinne looked at Venice. "How could you?"

"Don't give me a guilt trip, Corinne. I did what I had to do. No hard feelings. I'll even give you 24 hours to move your stuff out."

Tears rolled down Corinne's cheeks. She said nothing.

Venice disappeared upstairs and returned carrying her coat and handbag.

"Thank God I can finally get out of this place. Cabin fever!" She turned to Debbie. "I'm meeting Warren for lunch. I'll be back at the office by 3:00 or 3:30."

Venice walked out the door. Corinne closed it quietly behind her.

Debbie and Corinne gave each other a high-five.

33

Two days later, Debbie Towson moved into Apartment 18D, congratulating herself on the deal she'd made. She'd cleaned out her desk at Taft, Donohue & Calderon the evening before delivering the documents to Venice, and she hadn't gone back since.

The exchange had been simple but tricky. Debbie had called Warren Burgess's assistant Alana, with whom she was friendly, and who was as unfond of her employer as Debbie was of hers. Alana was happy to gossip, telling Debbie exactly what kinds of favors Warren had been calling in with Judge Herrold to secure the apartment for Venice.

Alana was more than happy to write the note and sign Warren's name; she did it often enough, and she had Warren's signature down pat. If anyone asked, Alana would say she had no idea how Debbie had gotten her hands on a piece of Burgess & Burgess stationery. In the meantime, Debbie dug out some old files and pieced together the language of Judge Herrold's "judgment," then got Alana to forge his signature.

In return for her services, Debbie got to move into the second bedroom of Apartment 18D for the duration of the two-year lease. She'd soon start interviewing for a new job, and with her skill set, she knew she'd have a position in no time. And with the money she'd be saving on rent, in a couple of years she could buy her own place. In the meantime, she thought she and Corinne would get along famously.

Corinne felt the same way. Her only regret was that she had resorted to the Tylenol P.M. tablets. But it had all turned out well. The others got a good night's sleep, and she got the apartment.

■ ■ ■ ■

EVERYBODY WINS

■ ■ ■ ■

1

They all looked around the apartment at their various piles of stuff, which they'd had no choice but to move in.

Corinne sighed and continued.

"Well, I guess the good news is, one of us gets to keep the apartment. But which one?"

"There's no way we could ever decide that among ourselves," Ian said. "We all want it, but let's face facts. We've been taken for a ride, and we'll probably all end up back where we started."

"We've *definitely* been taken for a ride," Venice declared, "but the way the lease is written, the occupant does have this apartment for two years at the impossible rent of $600 a month."

"I have an idea for how to make the best of this bizarre situation," Corinne said. "Unfortunately, none of us would get the apartment, but we all *would* end up a lot better off than we are now."

"I like the way *that* sounds," Oliver piped in. "What's your idea?"

"We all know this apartment would rent for at least fifteen grand a month, right? We also know there are always enough billionaires and trillionaires in Manhattan who are looking for exactly this type of place. So, we sublet it. Subtract the six hundred bucks a month that we owe, and that leaves us with $14,400 a month to split among us. That's what? About $3500 a month each. With that kind of money, I can get a much nicer place than the place I was living before."

"With that kind of money, I could go back to my old place *and* buy a car," Ollie said.

Venice considered the option. "I paid $1400 for my last place. I'd love to live here, but the thought of an extra three thousand dollars a month in cash is pretty appealing. OK, I've made up my mind. I'm in. All in favor, say 'Aye.' "

Four "Ayes" were said simultaneously.

"Perfect," Venice said. "You guys want to come down to my attorney's office, and we'll draw up the papers?"

"Let's go," Corinne said, grabbing her purse.

2

Corinne put her furniture in storage and slept on a friend's couch for three months. She found a reasonably priced apartment in a private house in Riverdale, a suburban section of the Bronx, where she lived for a year and dealt with the commute to midtown via express bus. After fifteen months, she'd saved enough money to put a down payment on a condo on the Upper West Side, which she'd never wanted to leave in the first place.

Ian was able to find a vacant apartment in the Washington Heights building he'd moved out of. After several years of trying to make it as an artist, he gave up and took a job teaching art at a highly regarded private school in Pittsburgh. He married one of the seventh-grade science teachers. Together they saved enough money to send their three children to art school.

Venice moved to Queens, then gave up

law three years later. With the money she'd saved subletting Apartment 18D, she packed up and moved to the west coast, where she opened a health food restaurant that has been voted California's best five years running.

Ollie moved in with his brother, then moved out three months later when they both realized that adult brothers shouldn't live together. He was lucky enough to find a small apartment in Morningside Heights, where he lived for two years. Tired of his job in network administration, he decided to pursue his dream of buying a car and driving across country. In California, he stopped at a famous health food restaurant and recognized the proprietress as a woman whose path he'd crossed in an Upper West Side penthouse several years earlier. They were married six months later.

■ ■ ■ ■

UNITED WE STAND

■ ■ ■ ■

into their respective beds,
om the day.

lay awake pondering the day's
ly in New York would four strang-
hemselves in a predicament like this,
ught. *The interesting thing is, I like all*
m, so far. So, in a way, the situation
t as bad as it could be. Which was
ething to be thankful for.

They all looked around the apartment at their various piles of stuff, which they'd had no choice but to move in.

Corinne sighed and continued.

"Well, I guess the good news is, one of us gets to keep the apartment. But which one?"

"Are any of us going to give up our claim voluntarily?" Ian asked, hoping against hope.

"You all seem like nice people," Venice said, pleasantly. "But I have to tell you, I'd give up a lung or a kidney before I'd give up this place."

"Ditto," Oliver agreed. "This is the only chance I'll ever have to live in a penthouse for six hundred bucks a month. I want to stay as much as you guys do."

"We have to figure something out," Corinne said. "But until we do, it looks like we're roommates. None of us are murderers, right?"

"Quite the opposite, actually," Venice said. "I'm an assistant district attorney."

"Struggling artist." Ian pointed to himself.

"Computer geek," said Oliver.

"Editor," said Corinne.

Venice looked around the room, then at the view of Central Park through the floor-to-ceiling windows. She sighed. "If we had to get stuck in a situation like this, at least we have a nice place to be stuck. I'm sure we can manage for a few days until we decide who stays and who goes."

"How do we split up the living space in the meantime?" Ian asked.

Venice had an idea. "Let's see, the apartment has four rooms, right? The two bedrooms, the living room, and the dining room. I have a screen we can use to separate the living room and the dining room. Maybe we should have a lottery to figure out who goes where."

"Sounds fair to me," Oliver said. "Even if I end up with the dining room, it's still bigger than the apartment I just moved out of. And with a lot fewer roaches, I'm sure."

Corinne and Ian nodded their agreement. Venice's plan seemed admirably unbiased.

Venice pulled a deck of cards from one of her boxes and shuffled it thoroughly. "High

card gets the master be___ ___est the second bedr___ living room, and lo___

"What about th___

"How about ___

"Spades are h___ monds, then clubs.___

Each of the four stra___ from the deck. Corinne g___ Venice pulled the 5 of clubs___ king of diamonds. Ollie ended___ 8 of spades.

The four helped one another move___ possessions to their new living quarters ___ Ian to the master bedroom, Corinne to the second bedroom, Oliver to the living room, and Venice to the dining room. They agreed that Venice, Ian, and Oliver would keep their kitchen utensils packed, since Corinne had already unpacked her kitchen things and they didn't need more than one set. They also decided that the first-floor bathroom would be for the men and the second-floor bath for the women.

By 10:00 p.m. their boxes were either unpacked or neatly stored in the corners of their individual living areas. They gathered in the kitchen and opened the bottle of expensive wine that Venice had brought to celebrate her new apartment. An hour later,

2

They'd agreed to reconvene the following evening over a pot-luck dinner to discuss a plan for moving forward. Corinne picked — up Japanese. Venice brought caesar salad wraps, and Ian brought fried tofu and veggies.

Venice melted when she saw the flimsy plastic bag in which Ian carried the two quarts of vegetarian fare. "You go to Buddhist Delight?" she asked Ian, delighted.

"You know it?"

"Know it? I practically live there when I'm working on a big case."

"Oh, are you guys vegetarians?" Corinne asked. "I wish I'd known . . . I got sushi and chicken."

"I do fish," Venice said.

"Me too," Ian said. "And chicken sometimes."

"But never beef." Venice and Ian nodded

and smiled at each other, as if at a secret joke.

Corinne looked at her watch. "I wonder where Ollie is?"

"We can't say 'It's not like him to be late,' since none of us really knows him," Venice pointed out.

"Maybe when we know him better, we'll be saying, 'Aargh, that Oliver — why can't he ever be on time?' " Ian put in.

"One thing's for sure," Corinne said. "He wouldn't want us to eat cold food."

The three temporary roommates sat around the kitchen table discussing various ways to determine who would get to keep the apartment. Occasionally they glanced at the front door, as if fearing that a fifth, sixth, and seventh person might enter and stake a claim.

Around nine o'clock they hit on an idea that could possibly have worked. Apartment 18D was rented on a two-year lease. If two people agreed to leave, the remaining two could agree to share the apartment. But that option still left the question of who would stay and who would go.

"We should probably wait for Oliver to get here before we discuss this any further," Corinne said, scooping some broccoli with garlic sauce onto her plate.

Ian nodded. "Agreed. It doesn't seem fair to make a decision without him." He'd barely finished his sentence when Oliver charged in.

"Dudes, sorry I'm so late. I was gonna call, but then I remembered — I don't know you guys, and I don't have your phone numbers." He looked at the kitchen table, at the dirty plates and the congealing veggies. "Uh-oh. I forgot to bring food. But I wanted to get back here as fast as I could. You're not gonna believe what happened today."

Corinne, Venice, and Ian all raised their eyebrows.

"OK, get this," Oliver continued, moving into narrative mode. "I'm at work this afternoon, and it's a really slow day, right? So I start surfing the Net, and I find this site about tenants' rights, et cetera. It had a lot of good stuff, and I wanted to print it all out to show you guys. But when I went to print it, my printer cable died on me. There's an office supply store a couple of blocks from work, so I figure I'll just run there, get the cable, and be back in fifteen minutes."

The others waited patiently for the story to get interesting.

"So I'm in the computer supply section

when all of a sudden I hear this voice. I definitely recognize it, but it's one of those voices you can't place right away, you know? So I listen and listen, and it still sounds familiar, but I still can't place it. So I move a little closer so I can see who it is. And even when I do see him, I still can't figure out who it is. It's like, I know the guy, but I can't think of where I know him from. So he talks to the sales guy a little bit more, and bang! It hits me. Guess who it was."

"Who?" Venice, Corinne, and Ian asked in unison.

"Are you ready for this? *Andrew Weisch.* The guy who rented us this apartment. I didn't recognize him at first because he shaved his head and now he has a goatee. But it was him all right."

Corinne's jaw hit the table. Venice's eyes widened.

"Wow," Ian said. He spoke for all of them.

"I didn't know what to do," Oliver continued. "I mean, I wanted to confront him right then and there, tell him he owed us three thousand bucks each and was he proud of himself for what he did to us? But there were a lot of people in the store, and I was afraid I'd get arrested or something. So I decided to follow him instead."

"You have guts, man." Ian smiled approvingly.

"I figured at the very least I could figure out where he was staying so that we could sic the cops on him. So I dropped the printer cable, and when he left, I followed him. First he took a cab to a health club, Crunch . . . it's about ten blocks from here. I pretended I was interested in joining the club, so they gave me a tour, and I timed it so that I could leave when Weisch did. So he walks to a restaurant on Amsterdam, sits at the bar and has a few drinks. A couple of guys showed up half an hour later carrying some sort of portfolio, but I couldn't see what was in it. The three of them had dinner, then the two guys left. Weisch walked to a swanky building on West End Ave. in the 90s. The doorman didn't stop him, so I figured he has to live there."

"I can't believe he's still walking the streets after what he did to Blackmore. And to us," Venice said. "Three of us are about to be homeless, and he lives in a ritzy building."

"Wait, there's more," Oliver went on. "I waited a couple of minutes after he went into the building, then I went in. I said to the doorman, 'Did I just see Andrew Weisch come in? I've been waiting for him.' And the doorman says, all snooty, 'There's no one in this building by that name.' And I go, 'But I can swear I just saw him walk in . . . the guy with the shaved head and tan business suit, carrying a portfolio.' And the doorman says, 'You must be mistaken, that's Adam Wendt.' So he must have changed his name, or he's going under a different name so the cops can't find him."

"I'm calling them right now," Venice said, picking up her cell phone. "If we time it right, we can be waiting outside his building when they haul him away."

"I have a better idea," Oliver said.

"A better idea? What's wrong with calling the police?" Venice asked.

"If we go to the cops, do you really think we'll get our three thousand bucks back? I don't know about you guys, but I don't wanna kiss my money good-bye."

"Me either," said Ian.

Corinne grimaced. "Me either. Moving into this place wiped out my entire savings account."

Venice sighed. "Mine too."

"Here's the bottom line, dudes," Oliver said. "We're sitting here broke, trying to figure out where we're going to live, and the guy who robbed us is living in the neighborhood and spending our money. If we want it back, we have to take matters into our own hands."

"But how?" Corinne asked.

"Simple," Oliver said. "We find a way to con the con man. With a team made up of an editor, an artist, an assistant D.A., and a computer guy, it should be easy."

The suggestion hung in the air as the room went silent.

Ian was the first to break the silence. "I'm in."

"Me too," said Corinne.

"Me three," said Venice. "I've changed my mind. No need to get the law involved. Except for me, that is."

3

Gallons of iced tea, bags of gourmet coffee, quarts of lo mein, and boxes of cookies were consumed as the Gang of Four brainstormed how to get their money back from the slippery Mr. Weisch/Wendt.

The kitchen became the official strategy room — the "war room," as Oliver called it. Corinne brought home a flip chart from work. Venice donated a bulletin board. Oliver bought a blackboard and a bucket of chalk at a discount store. Ian took notes and served as unofficial recording secretary.

The first step, they decided, was determining exactly how much money Andrew Weisch owed them. For surely he'd done more than $3000 worth of damage to each of them. Each of the four had to pay movers, and each would have to pay several months' security and rent when (if they were lucky) they found new apartments. Then they'd have to pay movers again *and* take more time off work (or, in Ian's case, turn down freelance work). Some of them had already bought furniture for Apartment 18D, and though they'd tried desperately to cancel their orders, their credit cards had already been charged and they were stuck with couches, loveseats, easy chairs, and bookshelves that would never fit into the tiny studios or one-bedrooms they'd end up moving into.

Of course, they also deserved compensation for punitive damages. "The disappointment of being promised a two-bedroom penthouse on Central Park West for six hundred dollars a month and then having to move out is surely worth millions," Ian pointed out. Even Venice, who'd seen juries award hundreds of millions of dollars for "pain and suffering" and who had no patience for such insanity, agreed that the four of them had suffered mightily and deserved a few bucks in recompense.

Ian got out his calculator and added up everyone's costs and losses. After some discussion, they agreed they'd be satisfied with $20,000 each. Having decided on the sum to be recovered, they turned to the larger challenge: figuring out how to separate Andrew Weisch from $80,000 in cash.

"There's no substitute for thorough research," Venice instructed. "It makes all the pieces fall into place. So, before we do anything else, we have to gather as much information as we can. I'll use my contacts in the NYPD to find out what's going on with the case. Ian, why don't you make friends with Blackmore's new assistant and see what you can find out? Corinne and Ollie — we know where he lives, right? I think you guys should stake him out for a few days, follow him around, see where he goes, who he hangs around with, what he does. Maybe that'll give us some ideas."

"But don't you think he'll recognize us?" Corinne asked. "It was a couple of weeks ago, sure, but he did sit directly across from us while we signed our leases. We don't want him to suspect anything."

"Well, he didn't recognize Ollie in the office supply place," Ian said. "But you have a point, Corinne. The good news is — I know a thing or two about make-up. I did one apprenticeship off-Broadway and another one with a fashion photographer when I was at FIT. I know a few tricks." He looked at Corinne. "Dark sunglasses and wigs can do a lot to make a woman mysterious, you know." He turned to Oliver. "As for you, Ollie, the first step is getting you some hair."

4

In her three years with the D.A.'s office, Venice had done many favors but asked for few in return. It was time to cash in some chips.

Her first step was to call Anthony Hernandez, a high ranking detective whom she'd dated briefly. The relationship hadn't worked out, but they'd remained friends and allies. From Detective Hernandez she learned that a warrant was active for the arrest of Andrew Weisch, who, the NYPD believed, had fled town.

Hernandez outlined all of Weisch's reasons for flying the coop. The information that Ian had gleaned from John Blackmore's new assistant, it turned out, was only the tip of the iceberg.

"The guy's a bad seed," Hernandez told Venice. "Over the last five years, he diverted millions from Blackmore's businesses into questionable charities. And the worst part is, Blackmore was like a father to him. Blackmore grew up with Andrew's father in Greenwich, and they were friends until Weisch Senior died ten years ago. Weisch's father never really amounted to much. In fact, people who know Blackmore think that he funneled a lot of 'anonymous' financial support to the Weisch family over the years. He even paid Andrew's college tuition. And this is what he gets in return."

"Any idea where Weisch could have gone?" Venice asked.

"Hard to say. He went to school in Bennington, Vermont, and he still has friends up there, but none of them have seen him lately. At least, none of them *admit* to seeing him. We've been watching the airports and we're pretty sure he hasn't left the country. We'll find him eventually. We have to, if you know what I mean."

"I'm not sure I *do* know what you mean. Is it getting hot politically?"

"Understatement of the year. Blackmore's putting pressure on the commissioner, who's putting pressure on us. We've even gotten extra manpower. Still a blank, though. And all I can say is, Weisch better hope we find him before Blackmore does."

"You think Blackmore's looking for him, too?"

"I know it for a fact. He's hired a couple of PI's to track Weisch down. We're not supposed to know about it, of course, but we do. If they find him, I'm not sure they're going to be . . . uh, 'gentle' . . . with him."

Venice changed the track of the conversation slightly. "What's this I'm hearing about a series of pranks Weisch played on Blackmore before he disappeared?"

Hernandez laughed. "You heard about that, huh? Pretty funny stuff. Sold the guy's Lamborghini to a Jersey kid for a couple thousand bucks, donated a hundred grand to the Ku Klux Klan in Blackmore's name, bought two camels from somewhere in the Middle East and had them sent to Blackmore's house in California. The list goes on and on. He must have sat up nights thinking about all the fun he could have."

"If Blackmore was so good to him, why would Weisch go out of his way to humiliate the man? Docsn't add up."

"Actually, it does. Weisch has always been a sort of 'arty' political type. He's got a real Marxist streak to him. Sees capitalism as the exploitation of human beings, blah blah blah. But he likes to live the high life, and he definitely loves money. And he seems to have some inside knowledge of things that went on in Blackmore's board room, things he didn't approve of. And, before you ask, I don't know what those things are. We're not allowed to ask, if you catch my drift. But even if we *could* ask, Blackmore's been doing this kind of stuff for decades. He knows the line between unethical and illegal, and he always stays within the law. Weisch knew that, and he decided that he could punish Blackmore better than anyone else. Or at least that's what his friends say. They're a bunch of freethinkers, too, a lot of 'em living in illegal lofts in Brooklyn. We got them to talk by threatening to send building inspectors over. More proof that the best way to get people to cooperate is to threaten to take away their big, cheap apartments."

"Heh heh," Venice chuckled uncomfortably, glad she was speaking to Anthony on the phone and that he couldn't see the expression on her face.

"Hey, why are you interested in this anyway?" Hernandez asked.

"Just curious. Read about in the paper and wondered what they were leaving out."

"Hmm, that's funny. Which paper? We've been doing everything we can to keep it away from the media. Blackmore doesn't want the publicity."

"Not sure," Venice said, thinking quickly. "It might have been one of those gossipy

New York Websites. If I remember, I'll send you an e-mail."

"How about lunch? I'm single again."

"Me too."

"Or maybe dinner for old time's sake."

"Which would lead to other things for old time's sake."

"And would that be so bad?"

"No, babe. But I kind of have my eye on someone."

"Oh." Hernandez sounded disappointed. "Who's the lucky guy?"

"Just someone who's living with me for a while."

"Huh?"

"Long story, Tony."

So . . . the NYPD had no idea that Andrew Weisch, a/k/a Adam Wendt, was still traipsing about the streets of Manhattan. That was good. But it also meant that the Gang of Four had to work quickly. If the NYPD didn't figure out where Weisch was, Blackmore's goons would. And then she and her new friends would all be out their three grand, plus a little extra for their pain and suffering.

5

Andrew's luxury apartment on East 96th Street, which he'd apparently vacated just a week earlier, was cordoned off with police tape.

Venice pulled the apartment keys out of her bag. She'd gone through a lot of trouble to get access to the place, and she'd be returning favors for years to come.

The door clicked open. "Come on," she said to Ian, who was wearing an NYPD jacket. He caught a glimpse of himself in a large mirror in the entry foyer.

"Hey, I look pretty good in this," Ian said, turning to the side to get a better look at himself.

"Don't be getting all cocky," Venice retorted, while secretly agreeing that he looked awfully cute.

"Come on, admit it," Ian flirted, squinting his eyes and trying to look sexy. "Women love a man in uniform."

"It's not a uniform, it's a jacket, and if anyone finds out that I borrowed it to break into the apartment of a man we're about to steal eighty thousand dollars from, it's going to reflect quite poorly on me."

Ian looked at Venice with admiration. "Venice, *nothing* could reflect poorly on you. As Ollie would say, you are one cool chick. One righteous broad. A totally rad and fab mama."

"Oh, please," Venice said, feeling a bit flustered. "I thought you only heard those cornball lines in singles bars."

"You know what I don't get? Every woman I know says that men don't compliment them enough. But when we do, we get accused of being insincere." He sighed heavily and dramatically. "Why do we even try, when we just can't win?"

"Oh, you can win. Or, at least, we can let you *think* you've won." Venice was tempted to grab Ian's face and smash her lips into his, but this was neither the time nor the place. She had to live with the guy for at least another week, and acting on what was clearly their mutual attraction needed to be back-burnered until Andrew Weisch got his come-uppance.

"OK, time to stop admiring yourself in the mirror, stud. Put your gloves on, and

147

let's see what makes our guy tick."

The apartment was a large two-bedroom decorated in an ultra-modern motif. They started in the living room, where all the furniture was black or white. Several man-sized abstract metallic sculptures stood in odd locations on the hardwood floor. The walls contained small and medium-sized niches holding pieces of sculpture.

"These look like Florianis," Ian said, picking up an eight-inch chrome block that resembled a cigarette pack with two cigarettes sticking out of it. He turned it over. "Whoa. It *is* a Floriani."

Venice knew nothing about art, having avoided humanities courses at John Jay College. "Floriani?"

"An older Italian sculptor who's finally getting noticed after decades of amazing work. He's had a couple of shows in New York, plus one in Paris and one in Vienna, I think. All of his pieces have been selling, from what I hear. Especially since MoMA added two of his earlier sculptures to their collection."

"What does something like this go for?" Venice asked. She took the block from Ian and turned it over in her hands, trying to see what made it more than a hunk of polished metal.

"Hard to say. I'd guess around two-fifty."

"Two hundred fifty dollars?"

"No, two hundred fifty *thousand* dollars."

Venice almost dropped the block. "What!"

Ian took the sculpture gently out of Venice's hands and placed it back in its niche. "Too bad we can't just walk off with this little beauty. It would fetch three times what we're trying to recover from Weisch."

"Forget it. We're here to steal Weisch's money, not his art. Come on, let's hit the bedroom."

Ian raised his eyebrows.

"You know what I mean," Venice said.

The master bedroom was sparsely furnished, with Asian-style furniture and small minimalist charcoal sketches hanging on the walls just below eye level. Ian exclaimed over the workmanship of the frames, then exclaimed again when he saw the signatures. "Unbelievable. They're Picassos."

Venice laughed at the series of kitschy photos hanging near the entrance to the master bathroom and in the bathroom itself. "Who'd put pictures of their mother in the bathroom?" she asked. Ian didn't mention that the photos were most likely original Cindy Shermans.

Other pieces of fine and expensive art by well-known or up-and-coming artists adorned the dining area and the second bedroom, which also served as a library. Custom-made suits and shirts filled the walk-in closet, and European shoes lined the floor. The kitchen cabinets held designer appliances that looked as if they'd been used only once, if ever.

"So that's how you live when you have too much money," Venice huffed as they locked the door behind them. She ripped down the remnants of the broken police tape, then took a roll of tape from her bag and began retaping the door.

"I have to give the guy credit, though," Ian said. "Excellent taste."

"You think so? The place seemed really cold to me. Didn't seem like a human being lived there. Just a robot, or George Jetson."

"I wonder if he bought that stuff with money he made legally, or just with money he stole."

Venice looked at Ian as if to say, *Could you possibly have said anything more naïve?*

Ian sighed. "You have to indulge me, Venice. It bothers me to think that the only people who can afford to buy art are the ones who lie, cheat, and steal. I guess I want the people who buy art to be as pure in their income and motives as I want the artists to be in their devotion to their craft. Bizarre, I guess."

Venice looked Ian straight in the eye. "No, Ian, it's not bizarre. It's admirable."

6

Corinne and Oliver met at Café 82 on Broadway to prepare their presentation to Venice and Ian. The two teams of roommates had been so involved in their research that they hadn't had much time to compare notes.

For the last five days, as Venice and Ian dug for insider information about Weisch and Blackmore, Corinne and Ollie had worked as a team to follow Andrew's comings and goings. The first morning, Corinne, in a wig and sunglasses, waited outside Andrew's building and followed at a discreet distance as he walked to his health club. The next morning, it had been Oliver's turn to stake out the building, and he too had followed Andrew to the club. It was enough to establish a pattern, so Oliver joined the club.

On the third day, Ollie was already in the club working out when Andrew arrived. Ollie's glue-on wig was quite uncomfortable, and he was happy to work on some of the Nautilus machines to keep his mind off his itchy scalp while observing Weisch.

Andrew did bicep and tricep work for a while, then switched over to the pec fly machine. Unlike many of the health club's other members, Andrew didn't seem interested in chatting with his fellow gymgoers or checking out the spandex-clad gym bunnies.

Half an hour after Weisch arrived, a young blonde woman in a white uniform came looking for him. He greeted her pleasantly, and the two of them walked toward the back of the club. Ollie followed and watched them disappear behind a door labeled "Massage Room."

An hour later, when Ollie saw the doorknob of the massage room jiggle, he made a beeline for the locker room. As Ollie undressed, Andrew walked in, retrieved a magazine from his locker, and made his way into the bubbling hot tub. Ollie took a long, long shower while he waited for Andrew to finish reading his magazine.

From the jacuzzi, Andrew went into the shower room, took a quick shower, got dressed, and left. Ollie placed a call via cell phone to Corinne, who was waiting near the gym entrance when Andrew emerged. She followed him for a few blocks and then lost him when he hailed a cab.

The next day, Corinne (wearing contacts instead of her glasses and a bandana to cover her hair) was waiting in a rent-a-car when Andrew emerged from the health club. He hailed a taxi, and Corinne followed as the cab made its way to a downtown restaurant. She miraculously found a parking spot, placed a call to Oliver, and walked into the restaurant, asking for a table for one. The hostess seated her a few tables away from the one at which Andrew sat with three other people, two men and a woman. The four friends drank wine and laughed. Corinne pretended to read her book but listened closely to the conversation, which seemed to be about politics. She heard the mayor's name mentioned several times.

Corinne's cell phone vibrated, her signal that Ollie had arrived. She paid her bill and left the restaurant quietly, handing the car keys and a note to Ollie, who was waiting outside and wearing a fashionable beret. Ollie read the note and retrieved the car. He watched from the driver's seat as Andrew's group emerged from the restaurant, then followed Andrew on foot as he separated from his friends and walked to Brooks

Brothers, where he purchased three ties and a pair of shoes. Corinne was waiting for Andrew when he emerged from Brooks Brothers. She followed him on foot until he grabbed another cab. Meanwhile, Ollie had returned to the Upper West Side in the rent-a-car to determine what time Andrew returned home on a typical evening.

"You'd think a merry prankster like him would lead a much more interesting life," Corinne said as she munched on her salad. She tried not to look too enviously at the burger and fries that Ollie was shoveling down with gusto.

Ollie caught her glance. "You want some fries?" he asked.

"Oh, I can't. Not good for the waistline."

Ollie shrugged. They exchanged a glance. Corinne thought, suddenly, *You're attracted to him, Corinne. Are you nuts? He's ten years younger than you, with a shaved head and a surfer dude vocabulary. But he's a sweetheart. And you could get used to that Mr. Clean look, couldn't you?*

"Anyway, where were we?" Corinne continued. "Looks like we have his life mostly figured out. Leaves the building around 10:30 to go to the gym. Gym from 10:30 to 12:30. Then lunch, either by himself or with friends. Then shopping and spending our

155

money. Back to the apartment around 6:00, out again at 8:00. Home between midnight and 2 a.m. Must be nice not to have a job."

"Still a lot we don't know, though. Like that tall chick with red hair he had dinner with, and went back to her apartment with. Girlfriend?"

"I don't think so. The body language wasn't right. I'd say just friends."

"Maybe we should watch her, too. She might know something."

"Let's ask Venice, but my sense is no. It's hard enough keeping track of Weisch. There aren't enough of us to stake her out, too."

"I can't get over this dude. Cops all over New York are looking for him, but he's still walking around like everything's normal. I thought for sure he was gonna buy something in that gallery this afternoon. Fifty thou for one weird piece of junk. It's messed up."

Ollie looked at his lunch, then at Corinne. He lifted the plate and with his fork slid about ten french fries from his plate to hers. "Go on, bud. You deserve 'em."

Corinne's heart thumped a bit louder as she dug into the starchy masses of cholesterol and fat. How could she say no to a guy who shared his french fries with her and described an expensive piece of modern

156

art, by a well-known artist, as a "weird piece of junk"?

7

They'd been calling in sick, taking personal days, and "working from home" since they'd arrived at Apartment 18D. Bosses and supervisors were starting to get suspicious. But the Gang of Four wasn't going back to work until they'd recovered their money. So they all took another sick day to stay home and plan their strategy.

They began the meeting (in the War Room, with a table full of Snapple iced teas and Stella d'Oro cookies) by talking about everything except Andrew Weisch.

After half an hour of conversation in which Weisch's name wasn't even mentioned, Ian said, "We're putting off talking about . . . the plan. Why? Are we having second thoughts?"

"No way." Oliver was vehement. "With the way that guy lives, I want to nail him more than ever."

Corinne nearly spat. "You have to see him

strolling around town like he's the King of Manhattan Island. It took all my self-control not to rip my wig off, reveal myself, and start screaming at him. Luckily, I'm not a big drama queen."

"I have a confession to make," Venice said. "I'm *totally* excited about what we're doing. I mean, this is vigilante justice, pure and simple. If word of it ever gets out, my career is down the tubes. But God, vigilante justice feels good. I feel completely energized. A week ago, if you'd told me I'd be plotting revenge with three strangers on a thief who did me out of my savings, I'd have said you were crazy. But I'm having the time of my life."

They all nodded vigorously, agreeing that some cosmic force seemed to have brought them together.

"I know why we're putting off talking about it," Corinne said. "It's because the easy part is over. We've found out everything we *can* find out about Weisch. Now it's time to take action."

Venice nodded. "You're right. Weisch can't stay at large too much longer. When Ian and I visited his apartment, we saw two guys staking out the place from across the street. They must be the guys Blackmore hired. They've probably figured out that Weisch is still in the City somewhere, and the second they find him, it'll be all over for us."

"Then may I suggest that we begin?" Ian asked. "Venice and I have some ideas we've been kicking around, and I'm sure you guys do, too."

"We definitely do," Oliver said. Both Corinne and Venice noticed that they'd been referred to as part of a couple, and neither minded in the least.

"Great!" Ian said. "You guys mind if we go first? We have a fabulous idea that we think could actually work."

"We're all ears," said Corinne.

It took them n...
arguing, and play...
by 10 p.m., they had ...

"The plan" was goi...
cooperation of many trusted ...
lies. But they knew they'd hav...
gathering the support they needed. ...
one of the great things about livi...
Manhattan. People would do anything fo...
free night out.

They had to move fast, though. It was almost Tuesday morning, and they had to make it happen by Friday night. They'd valiantly tried to figure out a way to have their money back in their pockets by Thursday; that one extra day could prove crucial if Blackmore's PI's were indeed closing in on Weisch. But they couldn't make it happen for Thursday. So Friday it was.

They got to work. The first step was throwing Blackmore's goons off the scent.

urs later, Venice found herself once
calling in favors to get the keys to
ch's deserted apartment on the East
e. She asked Tony Hernandez to drive
r to East 96th Street because she wanted
o arrive as obviously as possible, and an
NYPD police car seemed like the best way
to do it.

"You gonna tell me what this is all about?"
Hernandez asked.

"Of course not. I can't believe you're even
asking."

"If we get caught, I'm gonna be flipping
burgers at McDonald's."

"I hope you'll put in a good word for me
with the manager."

They pulled up in front of the building.
Out of the corner of her eye Venice spied
the same two guys she'd seen on her first
visit. She asked Hernandez to wait for her
in front of the building, saying she'd be back

in fifteen minutes.

After using Weisch's bathroom to freshen up her make-up — she had fifteen minutes to kill, after all — she emerged from the building and opened the passenger-side door of the police car.

"OK, Tony, look slightly behind you, to your left." Hernandez adjusted his eyes toward the rear-view mirror as Venice continued. "There are two guys standing by the mailbox. Slowly turn around and pretend to notice them. Then turn back to me and say anything you want. Talk for two minutes."

Hernandez did as instructed. After listening to her friend recite the alphabet twice, Venice nodded, shut the car door, crossed the street, and approached the two men.

She recognized the older guy as Sal DelVecchio, a good, if sleazy, PI with plenty of friends both in the department and on the street.

"Sal DelVecchio — What brings you to this part of town?" Venice asked amiably.

"Venice Calderon — I'm just mailing a few letters to my dear sweet Grandma."

"How *is* dear sweet Grandma?"

"Fair to middlin'."

"What a coincidence that you're using a mailbox across the street from Andrew

Weisch's apartment."

"Andrew Weisch lives around here?"

"What do you want, lady?" the younger guy asked, thrusting his chest out slightly.

"Who's the peacock?" Venice asked.

"Shut up, Vinnie," Sal ordered. Vinnie did as instructed.

"Sal, let's talk a walk, OK?"

"Sure, anything for you, Venice." Venice locked arms with Sal, and the two began strolling down East 96th Street.

"Here's the deal, Sal. You're trying to find Weisch, and so are we. Looks like neither of us is having any luck."

"You know they always go back home. He'll be here eventually."

"No, he won't. He's gone."

"Wrong. He's still in New York."

"Wrong. He's in Boca."

"Then what are *you* doing here?"

"Long story, Sal. Bottom line: Even when we find him — and we *will* find him — we can't touch him. He'll be out on bail in two days, and even if he goes to trial he'll never get convicted. And that really makes some people angry."

"Blackmore, especially."

"I'm talking people way beyond Blackmore."

"Who?"

"Can't say. But I gotta tell you, I'm in a no-win situation. That's where you might be able to help."

In his twenty years as a PI, DelVecchio had learned never to underestimate the inner political workings of the NYPD. "Anything to help a friend, Venice."

"It's so wonderful to see you again, Sal. I'm going to give you my phone number so we can stay in touch." She reached into her handbag, pulled out a slip of paper, and handed it to DelVecchio. He read it hastily:

Erte Hotel
125 Ocean Blvd.
South Miami Beach, FL
Check-in: Thursday
Check out: Saturday afternoon
Alias: Marco Piretti

Venice looked at the note, then at DelVecchio. "Oh, no!" she exclaimed. "That's top secret. You won't tell anyone where Weisch will be showing up on Thursday, will you?"

"I won't tell a soul," DelVecchio promised.

10

During their stakeout of Andrew's current West End Avenue apartment, Corinne and Ollie had discovered that the doormen change shifts at 4 p.m., 11 p.m., and 8 a.m.

As Venice was sending Sal DelVecchio and his young apprentice on a wild goose chase to South Beach, Corinne was waiting across the street from Andrew's building in the rent-a-car. She was dressed in her finest clothes, wearing her best jewelry and shoes, sporting an Edith Head–style wig, and carrying her most expensive handbag. Ollie was waiting around the corner, wearing a spiked-blond toupee, a grimy T-shirt with a deli logo, several temporary tattoos, and a few faux body piercings. He was carrying a white plastic bag filled with round metallic tins of breakfast food.

Ollie and Corinne had seen delivery guys from a Broadway deli going into and out of Weisch's building at all hours. The doormen never stopped the delivery guys, who, it seemed, walked right into the building, got into the elevator, brought the food up to various apartments, then left the building a few minutes later. It had been a simple matter for Ollie to catch up to one of the delivery guys, a young Latino.

"Bro, I love the Six Brothers Deli. Cool T-shirt. You know where I can get one?"

The delivery guy had heard stranger things. "No, I don't know, man," he said in a Spanish accent.

"I really like the T-shirt, bro . . . You interested in selling yours?"

Ollie expected a confused glance or a curt dismissal. Instead, the delivery guy said, "How much you payin', man?"

"I don't know, maybe 10 bucks?"

"These T-shirts go for 20."

Ollie nodded. The kid peeled off his T-shirt and handed it to Ollie, who gave him twenty dollars in return.

Ollie's next stop had been a uniform store downtown, where he'd used his close-to-maxed-out credit card to buy a white deli apron to complete the costume. If they didn't succeed in getting their money back from Weisch, his credit was going to be ruined forever.

He was now wearing the T-shirt and the

apron. When the morning doorman arrived, Ollie took advantage of the changing of the guard to enter the building. The two doormen, who were standing outside and chatting in a language Ollie didn't recognize, waved Ollie in. Looking quickly over his shoulder, he deftly dropped a note on the doorman's stand. Then he took the elevator to the tenth floor. On a previous visit, he'd been able to stand in the lobby long enough to check out the tenant directory and learn that Weisch/Wendt lived in Apartment 8A.

In the stairwell between the tenth and eleventh floors, Ollie removed the tins of food from the plastic bag and pulled out a change of clothes from underneath. Hoping that no one would enter the stairwell — and why would anyone possibly want to walk down eleven flights of stairs? — he changed into an expensive business suit that he'd borrowed from a stock broker friend. Gritting his teeth, he ripped off the spiky blond toupee and replaced it with another wig meant to simulate a short, straight Wall Street hairstyle. He tossed the metal tins and his delivery boy uniform into the trash chute on the tenth floor, then walked the halls quietly and nonchalantly.

Corinne strolled into the building confidently at 8:15. "Good morning," she announced. "I'm Lorene LeChanté. I need to get up to the penthouse floor, please."

The doorman looked at her quizzically. "Can I buzz someone for you?"

"That won't be necessary," Corinne said pleasantly. "I'm the building's decorator. I'm surveying the hallways to plan the new carpeting, paint colors, and corridor furnishings. Surely the management told you to expect me this morning?"

"Well, no. . . ."

"Would you mind checking?" She peered over the desk. "Oh, look, there's a note — maybe it says something about my visit?" She pointed to the envelope that Ollie had dropped on the stand.

The doorman opened the envelope. Inside was a handwritten note:

The mgmt. company called to say that a Ms. Loreen Lashantay is coming to the building in the morning. Let her go up stairs & provide her with any help she needs. She's the decorator. She may need a ladder etc.

"Go right up miss," the doorman said, ringing for the elevator. "Can I help you with anything?"

"I should be fine for now, but thank you."

Corinne got into the elevator and placed a borrowed wedding ring on her left hand. She got off on the twentieth floor and started a floor-by-floor search for Ollie. She found him on the fifteenth floor, and together they strolled the halls, occasionally riding the elevator from one floor to another. By ten o'clock they were on the eighth floor, waiting — praying — for Andrew Weisch to emerge from his apartment. In the meantime, Ollie rang for the elevator several times. When it arrived, he pushed all the buttons and sent it up to the penthouse, one floor at a time. They needed as much time with Andrew as possible.

At 10:12, just after Ollie had sent the elevator up to the twentieth floor for the fourth time, they saw the doorknob to Apartment 8A jiggle. They moved into place in front of the elevator, their backs to Weisch, and became a married couple engaged in an unpleasant dispute.

"Marshall, I'm tired of discussing this," Corinne said condescendingly. "You are *not* spending our money on something with no artistic merit whatsoever."

"You know what, Lorene? You don't know what you're talking about."

"*I* don't know what *I'm* talking about? You sell hog futures and soybeans, and you think *you* know more about art than *I* do?"

"Look, Lorene, I couldn't care less about the garbage that you consider 'art.' But I do like easy money, and so should you. Someone's buying your clothes and jewelry, and it isn't you."

"I don't approve of him, Marshall. He's derivative and commercial."

"Look, it's not like we're going to hang it in the apartment. As soon as he dies, its value is going to skyrocket. I'll turn around and sell it, and that'll be the end of that."

"I have an ethical issue with you using insider knowledge about someone's health to make money."

"Since when are you Ms. Morality?"

Corinne lowered her voice and simulated deep anger. "All right, fine. Do whatever you want. But don't expect me to go with you."

"You *will* be going with me. The only way I was able to get the invitation was by saying you'd be there. And if you don't show up, no allowance for you this month."

"Oh, all right," Corinne said, exasperatedly. "Where's the invitation? They won't let us in without it, you know."

Ollie tapped his jacket pocket. "Right here."

"Give it to me," Corinne ordered. "You'll

lose it." Oliver handed her a thick elegant envelope made of expensive handmade paper.

The elevator arrived. Corinne and Ollie turned around and "noticed" Andrew standing behind them. They stepped aside to let him into the elevator first, so that they'd be standing in front of him.

Here was the tricky part. Corinne pretended to slide the envelope into the side pocket of her bag, but instead let it fall to the floor. Neither she nor Ollie noticed; they just kept bickering about her snobbery and his lack of morals.

They reached the lobby. Corinne and Ollie left the elevator. Andrew Weisch did not.

11

Back at the apartment, Ian was busy assembling his favorite canvases. He'd chosen eight that he particularly liked and another eight that he liked somewhat less.

Venice had spent the better part of an hour helping him get into costume. With the help of theater paint, fake moles, and a wig of long flowing white hair, they converted Ian from a thirty-something blond in good physical shape into a sickly-looking senior citizen dressed in black from head to toe.

At eleven a.m. Ian's friend Robert arrived to take the photos with his digital camera. Robert was a perfectionist; each canvas had to be lit perfectly before he'd begin snapping pictures. He took numerous shots of Ian in his black gear. Venice, wearing Georgia O'Keeffe-type clothing and a wig that transformed her hair into a severe bun, was featured in some of the shots as the artist's humorless and long-suffering wife. Ian had to change clothes several times, because they also needed some shots of the artist "at work."

The photo shoot took more than two hours. Robert loaded the pictures onto Ian's computer and began manipulating the images. When everyone was satisfied, they burned them onto a CD-ROM and brought them to Ollie's workstation, hoping that he'd arrive soon to begin work on the Website.

Corinne and Ollie arrived a few minutes later, nervous but feeling that Phase One had gone well. Ollie handed the rent-a-car keys to Ian, who'd changed clothes (again) and taken off his make-up. Together, Ian, Venice, and Robert began hauling the canvases down to the car.

When the Ian/Venice/Robert team was gone, Corinne sat down with the latest issue of *Art in America* (she'd bought three of the same issue at the Barnes & Noble on Broadway). This magazine was, apparently, Andrew's periodical of choice. Venice and Ian had seen back issues lined up neatly in magazine holders in his East Side apartment, and Ollie had seen Andrew reading it while pedaling an exercise bike and later while sitting in the hot tub at the health club.

Corinne began writing the article, mimicking the magazine's style and thinking about the photos she wanted to use.

The nice thing about writing for an art magazine, Corinne thought, was the relative lack of words; such magazines were all about the pictures. Within 90 minutes, she'd written the article, revised it, and run it through the spell checker.

It was time for Ollie to work his magic. *Art in America* had been one of the first art journals to begin offering online subscriptions, providing art lovers and collectors with electronic PDF files via e-mail as an alternative to the printed and bound magazine. In addition to the copies she'd bought at the Barnes & Noble, Corinne had subscribed to the electronic version — at the hefty price of $250 for six issues — and had the latest issue's PDF files ready for Ollie.

Using QuarkXpress, Ollie formatted Corinne's article to match the others in the magazine. He removed the files for pages 52–60 (all advertisements) and substituted Corinne's article.

"Don't forget to add it to the table of contents, too," Corinne said.

When he was done, Ollie burned all the

files onto a CD-ROM, which Corinne placed in her purse. On her way out the door, she said, "Get cracking on that Website, Mister."

"Will do, boss. Hey, Cor?"

"Yes?"

"Could you bring me back some fries? I'll share 'em with you. . . ."

Was he the cutest man who ever lived?

12

The printer's shop was on a tiny street just off the West Side Highway. Corinne walked in and asked for Mr. Han.

"You are Miss Jensen?" the old Chinese gentleman asked.

"I am."

"You have CD?"

"I do." She took the CD out of her purse and handed it to him.

"OK, machine is ready. Sit, have coffee."

Corinne sat in a cramped coffee room with exposed asbestos-covered pipes. With an Xacto knife she'd brought along, she removed the covers from the hard copies of *Art in America.* An hour later, Mr. Han returned to ask for the covers. She gave them to him, and he returned shortly thereafter with the printed magazines.

"This technology is amazing," she marveled, flipping through the just-printed magazines. They looked and felt almost exactly the same as the issues she'd bought at the bookstore.

"Yes, but not cheap," Mr. Han said, smiling.

"Worth it, though," Corinne said, handing Mr. Han $1,650 in cash. She'd had to take the money as an advance against her credit card and wasn't looking forward to paying the 21% interest if she didn't get her money back from Weisch.

There was only one thing left to do. She removed the blow-in and subscription cards from the original magazines and placed them in the new versions. Surely anybody would be suspicious if a dozen annoying cards didn't fall out of a magazine as soon as it was opened.

Hmmm . . . that gave her another idea.

13

Venice, Ian, and Robert drove to West 18th Street in Chelsea, home of the oh-so-trendy Croyer Gallery. The Croyer's manager, Chuck Kristian — Robert's partner and a good friend of Ian's — had cleared space in the storage room. He helped unload the canvases, apologizing for the mess.

"It's always chaos back here when we're done breaking down a show," he explained.

When the canvases were safely stacked, Ian and Venice unlocked the trunk of the car and unloaded paint cans, dropcloths, string lights, and other decorating impedimenta. The shades in the gallery's front windows were drawn so that no passersby could watch the team paint and detail the gallery's two rooms in a manner that would best display the important work of Walter Licht. However, pedestrians who cared to look could see a small window box holding an elegantly hand-lettered placard on a delicate metal stand.

> *Friday Evening*
>
> *Walter Licht*
>
> *By Invitation Only*

Venice didn't know the first thing about displaying art, but that didn't matter; they wouldn't be hanging any of the paintings until the next morning anyway. Today's task was to paint, and painting required little or no training. The four worked in concentrated silence, talking only when questions needed to be asked or answered. There was no time for idle chatter. They had to get two coats of paint up today so that the lighting could be installed tomorrow and the paintings hung on Friday morning.

Ian had explained everything in his initial call to Chuck, and Chuck had assented immediately and vigorously.

"This is the greatest scam I've ever heard of. Or taken part in," Chuck said delightedly when they'd finished applying the first coat of paint.

"I think we're striking a blow for artists all over the City," Ian said. "If we pull this off, we'll prove that the artistic community wields a real-world power that society doesn't expect of us. They think we're a bunch of weirdos sitting in our lofts, dripping in paint and turpentine, out of touch with reality. This'll show them otherwise."

"It's great performance art, is what it is," Robert declared. As part of the deal, Ian and Venice had agreed to allow the whole evening to be videotaped by cameras hidden in the drop ceilings. Robert had vague plans to splice the footage together into a sort of documentary that he hoped would become an underground classic.

They ordered in Chinese food for lunch, then called for lattes and cappuccinos in late afternoon. By that time, the first coat of paint had dried and they'd begun on the second. They finished, exhausted, around midnight.

Chuck handed Ian the keys to the gallery so that he and Venice could return early the next morning. He also showed Ian how to deactivate the burglar alarm and how to turn the lights on and off, which turned out to be a tricky proposition due to poorly wired three-way switches.

"You guys head home, we'll lock up," Ian said.

"Gladly," Chuck said. "I'm exhausted, but excited. I cannot wait until Friday!"

"You'll keep a straight face, right, Chuck?" Ian asked.

Chuck opened his eyes wide. "You have nothing to worry about. The straight faces are absolutely essential. As Oscar Wilde would say!"

Venice and Ian cleared the dropcloths and did some general cleanup. Then they activated the alarm system and locked the doors behind them.

"Hungry?" Ian asked.

"Starved."

"Should we hit the diner?"

"Let's."

The only waitress in the Moonstruck diner showed them to a dimly lit corner booth. Venice slid into one side of the booth while Ian visited the restroom. When he returned, he slid next to Venice in the booth.

"You realize this is going to make it harder to talk?" she asked, her heart beating a bit faster. "We're going to have to twist our necks, and all that."

They kissed.

14

Sal DelVecchio was busy trying to glean information from the front desk clerk, an exotic looking, dark-skinned young woman with an unplaceable accent.

He'd arrived at the hotel first thing that morning, and he'd spent the last ten hours sitting in the lobby waiting for Andrew Weisch, a/k/a Marco Piretti, to check in. A succession of beautiful people had come and gone, but no Weisch. Could he have missed Weisch's arrival? DelVecchio didn't think so, but it couldn't hurt to make a few discreet inquiries.

"Sorry to bother you," DelVecchio said in the suavest tones of which he was capable. "I'm supposed to meet my colleague Marco Piretti here. His secretary told me he's checking in today. Can you tell me if he's here yet?"

The woman punched a few keys on a keyboard. "Mr. Piretti hasn't arrived yet, sir. Looks like he's been delayed — he'll be arriving tomorrow afternoon."

Rats, DelVecchio thought. What was he going to do for the next twenty-four hours? He didn't fit in among the South Beach set, but the hotel pool, which he could see from the lobby, looked extremely inviting.

"What's a room go for in this place?" he asked.

More clicking on the keyboard. "We have a vacancy this evening. A non-smoking room with a king-size bed and a view of the ocean; three hundred seventy-five dollars."

375 bucks for one night? What the heck — Blackmore could afford it.

"I'll take it."

15

Early the next morning, before Venice and Ian left for the gallery, Ollie gave his roommates a tour of the Website he'd been working on all night. Corinne had stayed up to give him moral support until four a.m., at which point she'd conked out.

Corinne, Venice, and Ian cooed with delight as Ollie walked them through the electronic pages. What a marketing tool for the Croyer Gallery it was — a special "preview" Website on which invitees could glimpse some of the Walter Licht paintings that would be auctioned on Friday.

The site wasn't live yet. To create suspense and heighten interest, Ollie had inserted a placeholder:

This Website will be online 24 hours only, from 7 p.m. Thursday until 7 p.m. Friday, when the auction begins. Please visit us at that time.

Ollie had wrangled with the Croyer's contacts at the Web hosting service to make sure that the site went live in time to support their plan. They'd had to pay an extra $1,000 for that assurance — a fee that was promptly added to Weisch's tab.

In addition to creating several "fan"-based sites for Licht's work, Ollie had also hacked into various art history databases and uploaded images of Licht's work, as well as a long biography of the artist that Corinne had written. Using several free e-mail addresses, he'd also posted comments about Licht's work to various art listservs and newsgroups. His goal had been to create enough links that a basic search on Yahoo, Google, or any other search engine would return at least a page of hits. All those links had been in place the day before he and Corinne had dropped the invitation in the elevator.

Ollie looked at his watch. "Yikes, I'd better book," he said. He was wearing a pair of sweat pants and a bandana that covered most of his head. In his backpack was the magazine printed by Mr. Han, and in his pocket were the keys that Venice had secured.

"Good luck," Corinne said solemnly as Venice, Ian, and Ollie left the apartment together. Corinne left soon thereafter to spend the day at an upscale caterer planning the cocktails and appetizers for Friday evening's soiree.

Planning social events is very nerve-wracking, she thought. She had new respect for convention and wedding planners, with whom, she decided, she wouldn't trade places for . . . a penthouse apartment on the 18th floor of a luxury building on the corner of 72nd Street and Central Park West.

16

Andrew was a creature of habit, at least as far as his gym activities were concerned. Over the last week, Ollie had watched Andrew's routine: lift weights or use the exercise bike for half an hour, get a massage, grab a magazine from his locker, sit in the whirlpool, take a shower, and leave.

Ollie was counting on that routine today, and Andrew didn't fail him. Weisch showed up right on time.

No sooner had Andrew left the locker room than Ollie pulled out the set of keys that Venice had obtained from Tony Hernandez. Despite his money (or, in actuality, *their* money), Andrew used a simple, inexpensive combination lock to guard his belongings. Ollie had scoped out the lock on several earlier occasions, noting the numbers etched into the back. He'd also noticed that the back of the lock contained a notch that looked like a keyhole. He'd reported this to Venice, whose detective friend had informed her that such locks were frequently used in private high schools, where principals were sometimes interested in getting into students' lockers quickly and easily. It had taken some doing, but Hernandez had managed to get his hands on a set of master keys for that brand of lock.

Ollie glanced around quickly to make sure that Andrew was indeed gone. To his dismay, a couple of guys entered the locker room and changed their clothes at the same bank of lockers in which Andrew's was located. Ollie kept cool, left the locker room, and returned a few minutes later, still clenching the keys.

The coast was clear. He unlocked the locker very close to Andrew's in which he'd stored the magazine that Mr. Han had printed the day before. The third key that he tried opened Andrew's lock. In one swift motion, Ollie reached into Ian's gym bag and pulled out the new issue of *Art in America* magazine (which Andrew had begun reading only the morning before), replacing it with their customized version of the same magazine. They'd placed postcards of Ian's work — Walter Licht's work — into the magazine so that they'd fall out when the magazine was opened. Both postcards, which had been printed on heavy stock on Ollie's laser printer, referred to the related article on pages 52 through 60.

Ollie slammed the locker shut, re-secured the combination lock, then jogged around the indoor track six times to work off some adrenaline.

At the end of his sixth lap, Ollie felt a sudden surge of panic. Surely Andrew was going to smell a rat. What if he decided that the work of Walter Licht wasn't worthy of attention, despite the private invitation he'd "found" in the elevator and the postcards that fell out of the magazine? What if he just skimmed the article, thus missing the several vague references to Licht's "declining health" or "reported illness, which the artist vehemently denies"? What if he looked only at the pictures and didn't read the list of major museums that had begun to display Licht's work, including MoMA, the Louvre, and the Prado? What if he didn't visit the exclusive Website listed on the private invitation that Corinne had dropped in the elevator?

Ollie timed it so that he'd be entering the shower room as Andrew sat in the hot tub and unfolded the magazine. Out of the corner of his eye, Ollie saw a slip of paper fall into the bubbling water of the hot tub.

Andrew retrieved it — the postcard! — and studied it carefully, then seemed to thumb to a very specific location in the first half of the magazine.

Ollie's lingering gaze attracted Andrew's attention.

Andrew looked him straight in the eye. "I'm not interested, man."

Ollie didn't know what to say. "W-what?" he stammered.

"I said, I'm not interested."

"Oh," Ollie said, forcing himself to remain calm. He smiled. "You're cute, that's all."

Ollie was back at the apartment twenty minutes later. He'd called Corinne on her cell phone earlier to tell her (1) that Weisch thought Ollie wanted to be his boyfriend, and (2) that the magazine placement seemed to have succeeded. Now, she leaned over his shoulder as he showed her the final Croyer Gallery Website for the Walter Licht auction, which had gone live an hour earlier.

She placed her hand on his shoulder. "Ollie, you are simply amazing."

Ollie turned his head to the right. They kissed.

17

Despite striking out time and time again in the hotel bar, DelVecchio enjoyed his evening at the Erte Hotel. Life was good when living it up at a client's expense.

The next morning, he positioned himself again in the hotel lobby and waited for Weisch's arrival. By six p.m., his quarry still hadn't arrived. At 6:15, the front desk clerk informed him that the hotel did not hold reservations past five o'clock and that Mr. Piretti's room had already been given to someone else.

The realization hit DelVecchio like a taxi cab. He pulled out his cell phone and angrily punched in a number.

Vinnie answered. "Yeah?"

"She played us."

18

The suspense was horrible. They kept as busy as they could. Venice and Ian worked at adjusting the paintings while Corinne dealt with the caterers. At two o'clock they all returned to the apartment to get into costume.

They'd been unable to decide whether or not the horrible elevator couple so convincingly portrayed by Corinne and Ollie should attend the auction. Having them attend seemed so . . . obvious, and they didn't want Andrew to get suspicious. And without their invitation — the one they'd "dropped" in the elevator — they wouldn't have been let into the gallery anyway. So in the end they decided that Ollie ("Marshall") would go on his own, and Corinne would show up as a different person, wearing a kooky downtown ensemble and dark eye make-up. Venice helped Ian get into his Walter Licht costume, then made herself into an elegant society woman in a tiny black dress.

They arrived back at the Croyer at 4:00. There was nothing left to do but wait.

Their trusted friends, co-workers, and family members — only those to whom they were very close, and only those who could keep a straight face — began gathering for cocktails at 5:00, the time specified by the invitation for the cocktails and viewing.

Chuck's assistant, Mykal, stood at the door examining invitations as people arrived. When a few curious passersby tried to enter, Mykal turned them away brusquely.

Corinne looked at her watch: 6:15, and no Andrew Weisch.

6:20, and no Andrew Weisch.

6:30.

6:35.

6:37. A bit of commotion at the front door. Corinne heard Mykal say condescendingly, "Sir, this reception is by invitation only. Sir. Sir!"

An uninvited guest barged into the room. Venice recognized him immediately. It was Vinnie Lorenzo, Sal DelVecchio's younger associate.

Being a good assistant D.A. means outthinking good defense attorneys, staying one step ahead of them every inch of the way. Venice turned and nodded to Ian, who nodded toward Ollie, who nodded toward the back room. Within five seconds Tony Hernandez was striding purposefully through the room and clapping his hand on Vinnie's shoulder.

"Hey, it's Vinnie Lorenzo," Tony said amiably. "What's a nice cat burglar like you doing in an art gallery? Sudden interest in the modern masters?"

"I'm minding my own business, Hernandez," Vinnie replied in a surly tone. "Quit hassling me."

"Didn't the gentleman at the door tell you this is an invitation-only event? You're trespassing."

"Fine. I'll wait outside."

"You wanna tell me about that little heist in Riverdale last week?"

Vinnie's eyes widened slightly. Hernandez knew he'd scored a point. The word on the street was reliable 90% of the time.

"Tell you what," Hernandez continued, taking Vinnie's elbow and steering him toward the front door. "You go back to wherever it is you live, and you stay there for the next three days. 72 hours. You don't call anyone, you don't have any visitors, you don't order in any food, you don't chat with anyone on the Internet. And I'll forget I saw you here tonight."

"Yeah, and how do I know this is on the level? That black chick" — he pointed his nose at Venice — "fed Sal a line and made him waste two days in Florida."

"You're just gonna have to trust me, Vinnie. You have five seconds to get out of my sight."

Vinnie thought for the first two seconds. By the time the fifth second had elapsed, he was gone.

19

6:40. Hernandez stood outside the front door making sure Vinnie didn't decide to make another surprise visit.

6:41. Ian waited with a flashlight at the gallery's back door. Hernandez didn't think Vinnie would be able to sneak in that way, but it made sense to have a lookout just in case.

6:44. Mykal stood aside as Andrew Weisch entered the gallery and began closely examining the paintings on the walls.

Of course he'd wait until 6:44. He was the only person who thought the event was real, so of course he'd be late, like a good Manhattanite.

Ollie exhaled deeply. He'd checked the preview Website an hour earlier and found that it had received eight hits. Who else could it have been but Weisch?

At 7:12 a small bell rang. Mykal locked the gallery's front door, and the art lovers walked up a flight of stairs to the second-floor auction room. Seventy-five chairs were available; all were taken. Walter Licht himself sat alone in the far left corner.

At 7:25, the first piece was brought in. Chuck began the bidding at $10,000. Ollie's mother, Kate, raised the bid to $15,000, only to be raised by Corinne's best friend, Jeanine Habel, who bid $20,000. They were both outbid by Jeanine's twin brother, Kurt, whose girlfriend liked "Composition #14" enough to get Kurt to pay $25,000 for it.

The second and third pieces didn't garner much interest. Ian fought feelings of hurt. He knew they weren't his best pieces, and everyone had been instructed not to overbid or go too wild, but he thought that *someone* should have taken the opening bids of $10,000 and $12,000 respectively.

The opening bid on the fifth canvas was $20,000, immediately raised to $30,000 by Chuck's friend Robin. Robin's ex, Lee, raised to $40,000. Ollie's sister Sandra raised to $45,000. Sandra's roommate Emma Logan raised to $50,000, and. . . . Andrew Weisch raised to $60,000.

In their separate seats, Corinne, Ollie, Ian, and Venice froze.

Ian's stepmother raised to $70,000. Going once, going twice . . . sold for $70,000.

Had they been too greedy?

The eighth canvas had been prominently featured in *Art in America* and on various Websites. The opening bid went up substantially; Chuck asked for $50,000 for "Blue and Green." Ollie's aunt Isabel walked away with it for $65,000.

The ninth canvas was one of Ian's favorites, an abstract titled "Revenge."

"May I have $60,000?"

Andrew raised his paddle.

"Sixty thousand. May I have sixty-five. Sixty-five?"

Corinne raised her paddle.

"I have sixty-five. May I have seventy-five?"

Andrew offered seventy-five.

"Seventy-five thousand dollars. I'd like eighty. May I see eighty?"

Venice raised her paddle — with a little too much enthusiasm, Chuck thought.

"I have eighty. Will someone give me eighty-five?"

Ollie raised his paddle and nodded.

"Eighty-five. May I have ninety?"

A miraculous thing happened.

Andrew Weisch said, "One hundred thousand dollars."

"I have one hundred. One hundred five?

One hundred five?"
Silence.
"One hundred once. Twice. Three times. Thank you, sir. Our next piece is. . . ."

20

After the auction, each purchaser met privately with Chuck in a small room. Andrew Weisch was the sixth person to pay. He arranged for immediate wire transfer of the money from "Adam Wendt" into the gallery's private account. Chuck took the address of the apartment on West End Avenue and arranged for delivery of "Revenge" the following Monday.

Andrew left the gallery looking very satisfied.

21

On Saturday morning, Chuck arrived at Apartment 18D with $100,000 in cash. The Gang of Four had ordered in a sumptuous, caviar-laden breakfast and insisted that Chuck celebrate with them.

They'd all agreed to give two thousand dollars each to Chuck, who refused to take a dime. "That was the most fun I've ever had in my life," he said, his jaw dropping open in delight at the eggs benedict. "I should be the one paying *you.*"

When Chuck left, they divided the money into five piles of $20,000 each. One pile went to Corinne, one to Oliver, one to Venice, and one to Ian.

Corinne looked up from her pile of money with a tear in her eye.

"I can't believe it's over," she said.

"Me either," Venice said, trying to stop her voice from cracking. "These last two weeks have been really . . . really . . ."

"Wonderful," Ian said.

Ollie took Corinne's hand. "Yes. The best."

"We have our money, and that's good. But we're back where we started," Corinne said, sadly. "Who gets the apartment?"

There was a moment of silence.

"Why don't we all stay?" Ian asked quietly. "Venice and I talked about this. We're happy to give you guys the master bedroom."

"And if we chip in for the rent," Venice added, "we end up paying only 150 bucks a month each to live here. And we get to be with our friends."

"Awesome idea, dudes," Ollie said. He looked at Corinne. "What do ya say, Cor?"

Corinne didn't have to think about it. "I say: Cool, dude."

22

There were just a few loose ends to tie up.

They still had $20,000 that didn't officially belong to any of them. After paying the project's expenses, they were left with an extra $5,785. Figuring that Andrew wouldn't miss the money — and that he'd be making quite a killing when poor old Walter Licht kicked the bucket — they made reservations at a Vermont bed and breakfast that Venice had always wanted to visit. They planned to leave for their New England getaway the following week, after taking care of one last unfinished piece of business.

After the vacation getaway was paid for, $1922 remained. First thing Monday morning, Corinne went to the bank and had a cashier's check drawn for $2,000, contributing the $78 differential from her personal funds. She returned to Apartment 18D, dressed up as her alter ego Lorene

LeChanté, and returned to the building on West End Avenue. The doorman recognized her and called the elevator for her. Five minutes later, on her way out of the building, she used her cell phone to call Venice.

At 10 a.m., Andrew Weisch entered the living room from the bedroom and saw an envelope lying near the front door. Curious, he picked it up and opened it. Inside was a $2,000 check payable to "The Andrew Weisch Legal Defense Fund."

"What the . . . ?" he asked of no one in particular.

There was a knock at the door. Andrew opened the door without asking who was there. Two uniformed NYPD officers stood in the doorway.

"Andrew Weisch? You're under arrest."

■ ■ ■ ■

Encore
Good Boys Never
Win

■ ■ ■ ■

So, you're probably wondering two things.

First, how did the saga of Apartment 18D really end? Did those four strangers really plot against one another for sole occupation of the penthouse? Did they sublet it and go their separate ways? Or did they become friends and work together to get their hard-earned money back?

Second, what happened with Corinne's job? At the start of our tale, you may recall, she was worried about her company being acquired and losing her job. Did she become a corporate survivor, or did she end up on the unemployment line?

Never fear. All questions will be answered in the pages that follow. . . .

1

Corinne Jensen threw herself onto the couch, exhausted. This was the second time she'd moved in two years, and she'd forgotten how exhausting the process is. In her last move, she'd gone from a small one-bedroom to a luxury duplex penthouse on the Upper West Side. This time she was moving from the penthouse into a Greenwich Village brownstone that she and her fiancé had bought with their two closest friends.

There's something to be said for letting life take you in unexpected directions, Corinne thought as she looked out the living room window, which overlooked pleasant little Leroy Street. *Two years ago, I didn't know Ollie, or Venice, or Ian. Now, I'm engaged to be married, and the four of us have just bought a house in the Village. It's all a little unbelievable.*

Unbelievable indeed. By rights, none of

them should ever have met. Corinne, a book editor for an old-world New York publisher, would never have encountered computer dude Oliver Pappas in her daily routine; nor would she have met Assistant Manhattan D.A. Venice Calderon or up-and-coming artist Ian McTeague. The four of them would have peacefully co-existed on the island of Manhattan, each blissfully unaware of the other three — if they hadn't all been swindled by a con artist named Andrew Weisch, who'd rented all of them the same apartment at the same time.

As it turned out, Weisch had actually done them a favor. The way the rental agreements had been worded, they couldn't be thrown out of the apartment until the two-year lease expired. Rather than calling their attorneys and battling it out for the right to live in the apartment — not that they could have done that anyway, as the move had left them all close to penniless — the four strangers had banded together to find Weisch and get their money back. In the end, Weisch had ended up behind bars, but not until they'd recovered everything he'd stolen from them, and then some.

But something strange and marvelous happened while the four singles, who'd jokingly referred to themselves as the "Gang of

Four," plotted and executed their scheme. Somehow Corinne and Ollie had fallen in love, and somehow Venice and Ian had done the same. By the time Weisch was in prison, they'd all become so fond of one another that they'd decided to live in the apartment together for the duration of the lease. The place was certainly big enough for the four of them, and at a rent of $150 a month per person the deal was tough to resist.

All four had saved their money in earnest for the duration of the lease, planning to use their savings to purchase co-ops or condos when the time came to leave Apartment 18D. But then Ollie had popped the question, which meant that he and Corinne could combine their savings to buy an even bigger, better place. Soon after, Venice and Ian proudly declared they were planning to buy a place together, too, and the two couples had begun apartment shopping. Corinne and Ollie had wanted to stay on the Upper West Side and were concentrating their search on quiet, residential West End Avenue. Venice wanted to be closer to work and Ian wanted to be closer to his fellow artists, so they began looking in SoHo and Chelsea. After a few weeks, Corinne and Venice decided not to talk about their respective apartment hunts any more; they would both end up crying at the thought of being so "far apart," one of those curious Manhattan phenomena that causes people located sixty blocks from each other to act as though they are living at separate ends of the earth.

But then, once again, fate intervened to keep the Gang of Four together. Venice had been assigned to prosecute a wealthy chiropractor who'd bilked Medicare out of millions. She'd gone to talk with one of the investigating detectives, Mike Grant, who was based out of the Greenwich Village precinct. Walking down Leroy Street on the way back to her downtown office, Venice had noticed a beautiful old brownstone for sale and, on a lark, had taken down the realtor's phone number.

Venice had called a meeting of the Gang of Four two nights later, in which she excitedly outlined her findings. The house, it turned out, was just that — a house, not an apartment building. It could easily be carved into two duplex units: one for Venice and Ian, one for Corinne and Ollie. The basement, which already had a kitchen, could be made into a couple of apartments to help with the mortgage. Yes, it was astronomically expensive — but not more expensive than what they'd be paying for other apartments in separate buildings. And the street was so lovely! And it was in the Village! Close to the subway! Near great restaurants! And quiet, so quiet!

Two days later, the two couples had gone back to the brownstone on Leroy Street. One week after that, they made their offer, which was accepted after only two weeks of haggling. And as of today Corinne and Ollie were the proud residents of the first and second floors of 28 Leroy Street, while Venice and Ian were the happy residents of the third and fourth.

From the corner of her eye, Corinne noticed a gleam of light. It could be only one thing: the sun reflecting off Ollie's bald head. Sure enough, Ollie was kneeling behind her, putting his arms around her neck and kissing her head.

"We did it, Cor."

Corinne sighed contentedly. Friends, love, and a beautiful new home. Who could ask for more? And she owed it all to Andrew Weisch.

2

After a week's vacation to move and get their apartments into a semblance of order, it was time for Corinne, Ollie, and Venice to go back to their office jobs. Meanwhile, Ian set up his studio in a renovated attic above his and Venice's duplex. Six months earlier, he'd given up trying to find affordable studio space in Manhattan and had taken a loft in Brooklyn. But when they bought the place on Leroy Street, he saw no need to renew the lease. Yes, the attic above their apartment was musty and hot, but nothing was closer to home. And if anyone asked, he could truthfully say his studio was a loft in Greenwich Village.

With a wince, Corinne nudged open the door to her office at Clarendon & Shaw. She flicked on the light switch and caught her breath. It was much worse than she'd imagined. Normally she'd return from vacation to a few dozen packages, but this time it looked as if every agent in America had found something interesting to send her.

She turned on her computer and began shuffling some of the Fed Ex and UPS boxes around while the machine booted up. A few minutes later, she clicked on her Outlook button and found 246 unread e-mail messages awaiting her. It was all too much. She fled the office in search of coffee.

She sensed something wrong as she negotiated the narrow, manuscript-strewn hallway to the mini-pantry, where the president's exceedingly stingy secretary, April Lagorda, grudgingly stocked the cheapest possible coffee and powdered creamers.

The hallways were just too quiet. Office doors, which were usually open even if the editors were hidden behind stacks of paper, were closed. Through the frosted glass of some of the offices, Corinne could make out the shapes of three or four people huddled close, whispering.

What could have happened while I was gone? she wondered. If anything major had transpired, her boss and good friend Martin Donovan would certainly have called her to share the gossip. Was the company on the block again? Corinne desperately hoped not; she wasn't sure she could stand another regime change. The management just seemed to get worse and worse, and the current regime — which had ruled with an iron fist for the last two years, since just after the dreaded merger — was the worst yet. If history was any indicator of the future, she thought, the next set of "leaders" would be direct descendants of Attila the Hun, using maces and battleaxes to destroy everything in their path.

She quickly poured a cup of coffee, hoping April wouldn't pop her head into the pantry and scare the daylights out of her. For an extremely large woman, April managed to move about the office like a cobra about to strike, quiet and deadly. Most of the time you didn't know she was upon you until she'd pounced.

Corinne sipped the coffee. Even though it was horrible, the caffeine flooded through her veins and gave her a rush of energy and confidence. On her way back to her office, she knocked on Clive Dudley's door. They'd started at the company only two weeks apart and had learned the ropes together. He'd acquired and published fabulous books that had reviewed very well, but he hadn't had any blockbusters and so hadn't yet been promoted to executive level, unlike Corinne, who'd been named Executive Editor just a year earlier, after *Troubled Love* hit. The promotion had been a preemptive strike to keep her from going to another house, and it had worked.

"Come in," she heard Clive say. She turned the doorknob tentatively and assessed the atmosphere. Clive was sitting at his desk, looking as if a heart attack were imminent. Their colleague Janet Massou sat at Clive's conference table looking equally anxious.

"Uh-oh. What's wrong?" she asked, not sure she wanted to know the answer.

Clive looked surprised. "You don't know?"

"Know what?"

Clive and Janet exchanged a glance.

"Martin's gone," Janet said simply.

"What?" Corinne couldn't believe her ears.

"Just like that," Clive said, snapping his fingers. "Here last Thursday, escorted out of the building on Friday."

Escorted out of the building. Yes, that was the way the managers of Clarendon & Shaw did things. When you left — whether on your own or at their request — you were treated as a common criminal. It didn't matter how many years of your life you'd given to the company, working 50, 60, 70 hours a week; it didn't matter how many successful books you'd published or the wonderful authors you'd acquired for Clarendon's prestigious and growing stable; it didn't matter that you did everything in your power to leave on the best possible terms. Once you were terminated from Clarendon & Shaw, you became persona non grata. April worked overtime to erase every last remnant of you, hiring philistines to clean your office and throw out anything you left behind. Within an hour, a new phone directory was circulated without your name, and your e-mail account was deactivated. Your voice mail message was somehow, miraculously, replaced with a mechanical voice directing you to call the operator for assistance. And that was the end of you.

Corinne sat down at the table with Janet. "What *happened?*"

"What do you *think* happened?" Janet asked bitterly. The bitterness wasn't aimed at Corinne but rather at the person all three of them knew was responsible for Martin's sudden departure.

"I'm not surprised he didn't call you," Clive said quietly. "He hasn't called any of us, either."

"He's probably embarrassed," Janet suggested.

"Or afraid of what he'll say," Corinne said. Martin was a sweetheart, but he was prone to the occasional explosion, a personality trait that hadn't endeared him to either April or April's boss, President and Publisher Victor Jennings.

"He's got nothing to be embarrassed about." Clive punched his desk softly. "Everyone should work as hard and be as talented as Martin."

Corinne and Janet nodded in silent agreement. Martin had trained all the younger editors, freely sharing his wisdom and experience with anyone who knocked on his door. If you weren't sure whether a young writer had the chops or the talent to make it, Martin would ask you a few simple questions that made the answer clear. He was a publisher's publisher, a man whose authors loved him and whose competitors respected him. He and Corinne had an especially close relationship. He'd hired her, trained her, supported her, and helped her become a star.

"Do we have *any* information?" Corinne asked, suppressing the urge to cry.

"Just that he got called into a meeting with Victor on Friday morning around eleven," Clive replied. "By noon, he was gone."

"We were supposed to have lunch that day," Janet said. "About 12:30, I went to his office. The door was closed and locked. His nameplate was gone. By the middle of the afternoon, the drones were here, throwing out his books and anything he left on the walls."

"This is just *unbelievable.*" Corinne felt her sorrow turning to anger. "How could they do this? This company *needs* Martin. Victor needs him as much as we do."

"And that's exactly the problem, isn't it?" Janet whispered ferociously. "Victor thinks he doesn't need *anyone.* We're nothing but spokes in the great wheel of Clarendon & Shaw. If we quit or leave, there are plenty of other people who'll take our jobs in the blink of an eye."

"I bet April was feeding Victor all kind of lies about Martin. Like she did about Nella."

"And Patrick."

"She's so evil," Janet spat. "What kind of person takes pleasure in destroying other people? She's like a Joan Collins character come to life."

"Can someone tell me how a *secretary* who can barely write a coherent e-mail ends up *running* a publishing company?" Corinne asked.

All three were silent for a moment. It was a question without an answer, one that everyone in the company had been asking for two years.

"You seem amazingly restrained, Clive," Corinne said. "You're usually good for a couple of zingers at April's expense."

Clive opened his mouth, shut it again, then shook his head. He looked white.

"Clive, what is it?"

"I . . . I . . ."

"Are you OK?"

"I haven't told anybody this yet. . . ."

"Are you leaving, too?" Janet asked. "You have another job? Good for you."

"Not yet."

"You're interviewing?"

"Not yet. I'm sure I will be soon, though."

"What makes you say that?"

Clive gulped. "Because Friday afternoon, after Martin was gone, I was sitting right here reading a manuscript. I looked up and there she was. April. You know how she just appears out of thin air. Our eyes met. She pointed her finger at me and hissed 'You're next.' "

3

No way would she be able to concentrate on reading proposals or manuscripts. She wondered, in fact, if she'd ever be able to read a manuscript again. Did Victor Jennings really believe the best way to motivate his staff to find and publish best-sellers was to fire a man they all admired? She doubted any work would get done at Clarendon & Shaw for at least two days, maybe three. Maybe more.

So she answered e-mail distractedly for a couple of hours, then checked her voice mail. Twenty messages were waiting — not too bad. The last message was from a familiar voice.

"Hi, Corinne. It's Martin. Could you give me a call at home?"

4

At noon the following day, Corinne stepped tentatively into 44, the restaurant located in the Royalton Hotel on West 44th Street. Chic and expensive, it is conveniently situated close to Clarendon & Shaw's midtown office. The fact that Clarendon, founded in crowded but charming office space in SoHo, had moved to one of Sixth Avenue's many nameless, featureless skyscrapers perfectly symbolized what the company had become.

I don't know how much longer I can give my life to a company that treats people this way, she thought as she took a seat in the bar area. For two years she'd been trying to keep her head buried in manuscripts, to remain focused on finding and publishing good books, whether fiction or nonfiction. But the atmosphere had become downright oppressive. At home Ollie listened patiently but always gave her the same piece of typically male advice. "Get out, hon," he'd say, matter-of-factly. "You work too hard to put up with this. The next time someone calls you for an interview, go."

She thought she'd do exactly that. The problem was: How did you acquire all these wonderful books and then leave your authors dangling when you abandoned them to go to another house? There was a special bond between editor and writer, but the writer's contract was with the publishing house, not the editor. It wasn't as if she could take her authors with her to Warner, or Random House, or FSG, or wherever she ended up.

She looked up from her glass of wine to see Martin standing next to her. He was a good-looking man, tall, silver-haired, and wiry, wearing his trademark tortoise-shell glasses. Corinne leapt to her feet and hugged him, holding back the tears. She wasn't usually a crybaby, but the whole situation was beyond upsetting.

The hostess seated them at a table in the center of the elegant open dining room, a location that couldn't have been less fortuitous. They were surrounded by colleagues from other publishing companies — Corinne spied a publisher and executive editor from Simon & Schuster at one table, an editor from Henry Holt at another.

"Look at them all trying not to look at me and pretending not to gossip," Martin said, ordering a martini.

"Well, I have to say, Martin, I thought it strange that you'd want to have lunch in such a . . . popular place."

"And why should I want to eat anywhere else? It's not like I've been convicted of a crime. I got fired by the biggest fraud in the publishing industry. It's a badge of honor, not shame."

The waitress delivered Martin's martini.

"Thank God these are back in style," Martin said, sipping his drink. "We used to have three or four of them at lunch every day. Those were the good old days." Martin cracked a smile, and Corinne's eyes widened in realization.

"Martin, you look wonderful. Relaxed. Happy."

"One would think you'd say that in a tone that *didn't* convey the onset of Doomsday."

Corinne fumbled for words. "I just . . . I mean . . . Oh Martin, this is so difficult. We all miss you, we hate what happened to you, we can't believe it. . . ."

"But my dear, this is a *good thing*. I was fired Friday morning, and Friday night I slept like a baby. I had a terrific weekend. Jeanne and I went to the cottage upstate.

On the way home we stopped to see my daughter and grandsons. I woke up today a happy man. The misery in my life is over, Corinne. Everything is good now. My only regret is that they made the decision for me. I should have made it myself, a long time ago."

"But *how* did it happen, Martin? What did they say? What reason did they give you?"

"There are the stated reasons, and there are the real reasons. Which would you like first?"

"The stated."

"Reason number one: Clarendon & Shaw is having a 'bad year' and is not going to make the 'number' promised to our monolithic Hong Kong–based parent company. Reason number two: Heads must be cut. Reason number three: They are very sorry, but my list didn't perform up to expectations last year, despite a blockbuster performance for the thirty-seven years prior to that. Reason number four: I am too highly paid to turn in lackluster performance. Reason number five: My insubordination with regard to personnel matters will no longer be tolerated."

"Victor said all this to you?"

"In exactly those words, in that icy tone of his. And April smiled triumphantly as I walked out the door."

Corinne grimaced. "And the real reasons?"

"You know the *real* reasons. April decided I need to go. So I went."

"You think this has something to do with the filing cabinets?"

"Can there be any doubt?"

Because their space was so new and modern, the offices of Clarendon & Shaw had ample filing space — so many vertical filing cabinets, in fact, that more than half of them remained unused. When they'd moved into the Sixth Avenue building a few months earlier, April had parceled out a paltry number of cabinets to each of the staff, reserving a large block for future use. When Martin ran out of filing space, he began using some of the empty cabinets. The following day, he received an e-mail from April ordering him to remove his unauthorized materials from the file drawers and to complete the Filing Cabinet Requisition Form. He'd deleted the e-mail, and two mornings later he'd arrived to find all his files on the floor of his office and the unauthorized filing cabinets locked.

Martin had flown angrily into Victor's office to complain — not for the first time — about Victor's overpaid, malicious secretary, who had the audacity to treat one of the most successful publishers in the industry like a first-year editorial assistant, or worse. As always, Victor had taken April's side, telling Martin that procedures had to be followed and that he could have the filing space he needed if he'd just fill out the Requisition.

Martin had swallowed his pride and filled out the form, only to be granted two small drawers of space. So Martin had used his expense account to buy a large vertical filing cabinet from Staples, which he'd had delivered directly to his office. April had tried to stop the deliverymen from leaving the cabinet in Martin's office, threatening to call security if they didn't take their delivery whence it came. But by that point the cabinet was already off the dolly. One of the deliverymen whispered something to the other one, perhaps an unflattering comment about April; the second one laughed; and April stalked off in a rage.

But of course that wasn't the end of it. The next morning Martin had walked into his office to find the filing cabinet gone and his files thrown — not placed carefully — onto the floor. April had clearly worked overtime to get the contraband filing cabinet out of the office. She'd also ordered Auditing to disallow the cost of the filing cabinet on Martin's expense report.

And then Martin had made his fatal mistake. He'd picked up the phone and called the CEO of HGSG, the multinational corporation that had purchased Clarendon & Shaw two years earlier. Having developed quite a good relationship with the CEO, Harry Hsin, at various meetings and company functions, Martin thought Harry might be able to help solve his problem.

"Harry," Martin had said, in his direct way, "you want me publishing best-sellers, right? I need filing space to do that, and I can't seem to get it. . . . To tell you the truth, I don't know why. There are at least 100 empty file drawers here in the office, but every time I try to use one of them I'm told I'm not 'permitted' to store my files in there. Who's telling me that? April . . . Yes, Victor's secretary. Well, I don't know, Harry, it's a mystery to me, too. Yes, I *have* talked to him about this . . . No, I still don't have what I need, and I must say it is a bit frustrating."

The next day, Martin had received a curt e-mail from April telling him he'd been granted access to file drawers 210–225. These were, of course, located in the bank of filing cabinets as far from his office as possible.

"Everyone admires the way you handled it, Martin," Corinne said.

"There's no way I could have gotten away with it, Corinne. Standing up to bullies on the playground works, but April and Victor aren't bullies. They're much worse. They're corporate survivors. They're like cockroaches. No matter what you do, you can't kill them. There was no way Victor was going to let me get away with making him lose face with Harry Hsin. So here I sit, sipping a martini with a dear friend and feeling content. Yes, content, but also filled with venomous rage and a desire for revenge against those evil beings."

"That's the word Janet used to describe April yesterday. Evil."

"It's not an exaggeration. Anyone who takes pleasure in hurting others *is* evil."

Corinne remembered something Martin had mentioned earlier in the conversation. "What did Victor mean when he said you'd been insubordinate in a personnel matter?"

A cloud crossed Martin's face. "Suffice it to say that Victor has been wanting me to fire someone for the last six months, and I've refused to do it."

"Who?"

Martin grimaced.

"Tell me, Martin."

"Clive."

Corinne caught her breath. *She pointed her finger at me and whispered "You're next."*

"But why?"

"Why do you think? April doesn't like him. He left the lights on in his office overnight a few times, so she thinks he cost the company money in wasted electricity. She caught him copying a manuscript on one side only instead of making double-sided copies. He used Fed Ex Overnight instead of UPS Ground a few times. So a few months ago, Victor started 'suggesting' Clive is a weak link and that we can do a lot better. I told him that was a bunch of bunk and showed him Clive's numbers. Finally, last week, he came right out and told me to fire him. I refused. And that gave him the perfect excuse."

"I just can't believe this, Martin. Is anybody safe? Am *I* even safe? April doesn't like me any more than she likes Clive. She still blames me for what happened with *Troubled Love.* As if I could know that Kaz Kazinski and Theo Resnick had made the whole thing up."

"That was as much my fault as yours, Corinne. I should have smelled a rat. But

231

Kaz is good, and who would have guessed what he was up to? As for April, she doesn't like *anyone.* When you gaze upon Miss April Lagorda, you gaze upon a truly wretched creature wrought by Beelzebub. She is joyless, angry, and miserable. And, as the saying goes, misery loves company."

"So what are you going to do now, Martin? Retire? Get another job? Write your memoirs?"

The coffee and desserts arrived.

"Well, since you asked," Martin said, pouring a shot of Sambuca into his coffee, "there's something I'd like to do before any of that. But I'll need your help."

"Of course, Martin. Anything."

"I'm sure you recall the scam you and your friends pulled to get your money back from that swindler."

"Recall it? We all think it was our finest moment!"

"Have you ever thought about doing it again?"

"Doing what again?" Corinne asked, confused. "The guy's in jail, serving ten years, I think."

"No, I mean banding together with your friends to help another friend. Because, Corinne, I have to tell you, if we don't do something about this situation, Clive is going to be without a job very soon. So is Janet, so is Meryn, so is Gian. We can't let Victor and April decimate a proud and wonderful publishing house."

"But what can *we* do about it?"

"You and your friends proved yourselves very competent in doling out poetic justice a couple of years ago. I'm sure you can do it again, just as effectively. Because you know it as well as I do, Corinne. *Victor and April must be stopped.*"

5

"Thank you so much for everything," Jeanne Donovan said graciously, kissing Corinne's cheek before moving on to Venice's. "Such a pleasure to meet you! You all must come upstate very soon. We have enough beds for everyone."

"We'd love to," Ian said, shaking Martin's hand while Ollie took his turn at kissing and being kissed by Jeanne.

"You must come too, Clive," Jeanne ordered. "We need at least one person who can beat Martin at tennis."

"It's not even a challenge," Clive said with a smile. It was the first time Corinne had seen him smile in a week.

Martin and Jeanne filed out, followed by Clive. All had volunteered to help straighten up and wash the dishes, an offer that Corinne and Venice had flatly refused. Of course they didn't expect their dinner guests to help with the clean-up. But, more than that, they didn't want them privy to the after-dessert conversation.

Ollie and Ian flopped themselves into prone positions, Ian on the couch (because he was taller) and Ollie on loveseat (because he was shorter). This was a system they'd worked out when all four of them had lived in the penthouse on Central Park, and it still served them well. Corinne and Venice loaded plates and glassware into the dishwasher, then joined their significant others in the living room. Ollie made room for Corinne on the loveseat, and Ian did the same for Venice on the couch.

"Guys, no falling asleep yet," Venice ordered. "It's only 10 o'clock."

"But I'm so *full*," Ollie whined.

"As am I," Ian said.

"Maybe you shouldn't have had that third glass of wine, dearest," Venice mock-scolded Ian, who responded by grabbing Venice's hand and intertwining his fingers with hers. A sculpted replica of their intertwined hands sat in the corner of their living room on the fourth floor, Ian's paint-encrusted thick fingers merging with Venice's long, sensuous, ebony fingers. Several collectors had offered Ian quite handsome sums for the piece at various shows over the last few months, but he'd never allow the piece to be sold — much to the frustration of the shows' sponsors.

"Those guys are totally cool," Ollie stated matter-of-factly, throwing his arm around Corinne. Declaring someone *cool* was the highest compliment Ollie could give that person. Ollie also indicated approval with such terms as *rad, awesome,* and *genius.* Woe betide you if Ollie considered you a *doofus, dweeb,* or *dingus.*

"What did *you* think of them?" Venice asked Ian.

A red flag went up. Venice always chose her words with extreme prosecutorial care, and Ian had learned, through experience, when Venice had an agenda. "All right, what's this all about?" he asked.

Ollie's radar screen had started to blip, too. "You're right, E," he said to Ian. "These two are up to something."

"You both are highly suspicious individuals," Venice said lightly.

"Well," Corinne admitted, "we do have something to discuss with you guys. . . ."

"We're listening," Ian said. Both he and Ollie were fully awake now.

So Corinne launched into her story. She went on at length about the way April was making life miserable for the entire Clarendon & Shaw staff, then angrily related her litany of complaints against Victor Jennings, whose sole goal seemed to be the destruction of a venerable old publishing company. She talked about how Clive's head was next on the chopping block and how hers might not be far behind.

Ian listened in shock. As a freelance artist, he'd never had to contend with corporate shenanigans and infighting, though he'd grown accustomed to a different brand of insanity in the art world. In contrast, Ollie, who'd worked in computer systems for some of the largest companies in Manhattan, nodded knowingly, not the least bit surprised by what he was hearing.

Corinne ended by recounting the details of her conversation with Martin at Restaurant 44. "He ended the lunch by saying that April and Victor have to be stopped, and he suggested that we might be able to help."

"*We* meaning you and Martin, or *we* meaning the four of us?" Ian asked.

"The four of us," Corinne responded. "Martin knows how we got our money back from Andrew Weisch and how we got him thrown in jail. He thought we might hatch a similar plot to get rid of April and Victor."

A silence filled the room. Corinne plowed on. "And I started thinking about it. He's absolutely right that something needs to be done. And maybe we *are* the ones to make it happen. So I floated the idea past Venice, and. . . ."

"And I'm totally in favor of it," Venice said adamantly. "I see things like this happen all the time in the D.A.'s office, and I'm tired of not being able to do anything about it. I'm sick of seeing the little guy get stepped on while some incompetent power-monger and his Satanic secretary climb the ladder."

"I'll admit that it sounds intriguing," Ian said cautiously. "The Weisch thing was quite an adventure. . . ."

It was Ollie's turn to speak. "Yo, not so fast, E. You guys are forgetting a few things. First, the only reason we did all that was to get our money back. Second, we would have been totally bankrupt if any of it backfired, which it could have, at any minute. We got lucky last time, guys. Everything worked out. There's no guarantee it would work *this* time, and then Corinne might end up getting fired."

"And would that really be so bad?" Corinne asked. "If we can't get rid of Victor and April, I'm going to start looking for a new job anyway. So I've got nothing to lose."

"What about you, Ven?" Ollie asked. "Last time around, you were all worried about your reputation. 'I'm a New York City prosecutor, my career is over if anyone finds out,' blah blah blah."

Venice waved a hand dismissively. "No one's going to find out. We were careful last time, and we'll be careful this time, too."

"If you're in, I'm in," Ian said to Venice, remembering the wonderful adrenaline rushes of their first plot and the months of artistic inspiration that had followed its successful execution.

"What do you say, Ollie?" Corinne asked.

Ollie looked at Corinne, at her soulful brown eyes that were made slightly smaller by her eyeglasses. "Like I'm going to be able to say no to you? I'm in. But can I ask a question? What exactly are we trying to accomplish? What's the plan?"

"If I recall correctly — and I do — we didn't start out with a plan to get back at Weisch," Venice said. "We sat down one night with some pizzas, started brainstorming, and figured it all out."

"So when does the brainstorming begin?" Ian asked.

"Tomorrow night at our place?" Venice suggested.

"We'll bring the pizza," Corinne said.

6

Corinne wished that all her brainstorming sessions could be as fruitful as the one she, Ollie, Venice, and Ian conducted to plot the downfall of Victor Jennings and April Lagorda.

After eight hours of psychological strategizing over pepperoni pies, micro brews from Ollie's favorite pub on Sullivan Street, a few bottles of Riesling, and Chinese take-out, they had their plan. Like the last time, each of the four had a role to play. And, like the last time, they'd need a few cameo appearances from various friends and supporters to make it all work.

Though it was 3 a.m., Venice was glowing with energy. "I can't wait to get started," she said, as they tossed the leftover pizza into the trash bin. "Looks like the Gang of Four is back in business."

"Oh, we forgot to open the fortune cookie," Corinne said, as she piled the leftover Chinese food into the refrigerator. She handed the cookie to Venice. "Would you do the honors?"

Venice cracked open the cookie as the other three waited to hear whether their plot would succeed or fail.

"Man who lie give big help for you and friend," Venice read.

Ian spoke for all of them. "Now how would a fortune cookie know *that?*"

For the fortune cookie seemed to be indicating support for the course of action they'd chosen.

7

Later that morning, Venice placed a call to the midtown precinct in which Clarendon & Shaw's offices were located. She asked to speak with the chief of police, Lou Geraldi, with whom she'd enjoyed a long-time friendship. Lou was a homeboy; he and Venice had been raised only a few blocks apart in Maspeth, Queens, and had attended the same senior prom (though not together).

"What do you want, Calderon?" Geraldi asked jokingly.

"A polite and friendly greeting would be a good start."

"Right, right, CPR. I sometimes forget." CPR is the motto that appears on all New York City police cars: Courtesy, Professionalism, Respect.

The two friends joked and traded gossip for a few minutes before Venice casually launched into her reason for calling.

"Listen, Lou, sometime within the next

couple of days you're going to get a call from a publishing company on Sixth Ave., Clarendon & Shaw. Instead of sending someone over there, I need you to call me instead."

Geraldi thought he knew exactly what was going on. "Sting?"

"In a manner of speaking."

"Can you give me details?"

"Not right now. Hush hush, and all that. I'll fill you in when all's said and done."

"You got it." Geraldi had been around as long as Venice and knew how to play the game.

"You have my number, right, Lou?"

"Memorized."

"Take it anyway," Venice said, giving him her cell number. "Call me as soon as you hear from them, OK?"

"You're the boss."

"Good man."

Geraldi remembered something he'd heard through the grapevine. "Hey, what's this about you marrying some artist? Never thought you went for the artsy type."

"Neither did I, but apparently I do. No marriage yet, but definitely the real thing. We just bought a place on Leroy Street."

"Good for you. I hope he knows what a catch he got."

"I remind him every day."

"Why don't the two of you come over for dinner one of these nights? Stella's always complaining that we never have any company since she popped out the kids."

"Would love to. I'll call you in a few weeks?"

"You'd better."

Venice hung up the phone, congratulating herself on getting Lou's help without telling him any lies. And if Lou wanted to assume the sting operation was conducted by the Prosecutor's office, who was she to correct his misperception?

8

"Yo, Hilda," Ollie called out to his boss, the director of IT. "You mind if I borrow one of the loaners for a couple of weeks? My machine at home is messed up."

They always kept more than enough loaners on hand to lend out to traveling or visiting executives. They'd never run out before, and Hilda doubted there'd be a run on the laptops any time soon.

"Just sign it out," Hilda said casually. To make sure Ollie wouldn't consider her a soft touch, she added, "But if anyone needs it, we might need to call it in."

9

It seemed a burglar was lurking in the halls of Clarendon & Shaw.

On Monday, Janet returned to her office after a meeting to find the contents of her purse spilled on the floor and her wallet missing. On Tuesday, Clive went to the coat closet at noon to retrieve his newly purchased (and expensive) leather coat, only to find it gone. Late Tuesday afternoon, Janet's fate also befell Corinne: Her purse, which she knew she'd locked in her desk drawer, had simply vanished into thin air.

Such petty thievery is not uncommon in Manhattan office buildings. Despite security systems with electronic key access, thieves often find it easy to sneak into office space and abscond with people's cash or clothing. The thefts usually occur late in the morning or around lunch time, when fewer employees are around to notice a stranger in their midst.

In accordance with company policy, Janet reported the theft to April, who promptly sent out an e-mail to the entire Clarendon & Shaw staff, who were housed on two floors connected by an interior staircase.

To: Clarendon & Shaw Employees
Fr: April Lagorda
Subject: THEFT
To everyone, today an employee had her wallet stolen from her office, it contained approx. $150 in cash & several credit cards. I remind all of you to ALWAYS LOCK UP your personnal belongings and to NOT bring any valuabbles to the office. If you saw anyone sussipicious looking on the premisses anytime today, please contact me.

The day after the theft of Clive's coat and Corinne's purse, April sent another e-mail.

To: Clarendon & Shaw Employees
Fr: April Lagorda
Subject: MORE THEFT
Do any of you ever read your email. Today two more employees had materials stolen. LOCK YOUR OFFICES when you are not in them and DO NOT bring valuabbles to work. DO NOT let

anyone into our offices if you do not reccognize them. ALL visitors must go through the reception desk on the 17th fl. IF YOU SEE anyone unfammiliar, report it to me immediately.

But April's dander was not fully raised until Wednesday, when Cal Ziotis, Director of Production and longtime April detractor, returned from lunch to find that his new laptop had been stolen off his desk. He had no idea how it could have happened, he said to April as she berated him for his carelessness. He'd locked his office door AND locked the laptop to his desk. But someone had managed to pick the door lock and then saw through the cable that fastened the machine to his desk. What was he supposed to do, he asked snidely, handcuff his computer to his arm and carry it everywhere with him?

A few peons having their wallets stolen was one thing. A thief making off with a corporate asset was quite another. After stalking the halls of the seventeenth and eighteenth floors for nearly two hours, flinging open the door to every closet and storage area in an attempt to catch the thief red-handed, April placed a call to the local precinct to report a rash of robberies.

10

While April grudgingly processed the paper-work required to purchase Cal a new laptop — for how, really, could the Director of Production be expected to go without a computer? — Cal made do with a slightly older laptop that he'd borrowed from a friend.

Fortunately, that friend had transferred all the files from Cal's stolen computer to the loaner computer the night before, so Cal was able to keep working as if nothing had ever happened. He'd watched in fascination as Ollie had worked his technomagic to make sure that Cal's work life would be unaffected by his participation in the plot.

The next morning — the day on which his computer would officially be "stolen" — Cal had simply carried his empty laptop bag into the office as if it contained his Clarendon-provided computer, which was actually snugly hidden on the top shelf of

his bedroom closet. And there it would
remain until Victor and April were gone.

11

The Clarendon & Shaw receptionist looked up to see an attractive young black woman standing in front of her.

"I'm Detective Calderon, NYPD," Venice said, flashing what looked like a badge. "I'm here to see April Lagorda, please."

The receptionist, who served at April's pleasure and lived in fear of her wrath, hurried to ring April's line. A few moments later, April's imminent arrival was signaled by a thunderous stamping that shook the small vase of delicate flowers on the reception desk.

Venice's first thought was: *Good Lord, Corinne wasn't exaggerating.* If anything, Corinne's descriptions of April as a hideous beast didn't do justice to Miss April Lagorda.

"This way," April commanded, then turned heel so that Venice could follow her down the narrow hallway to April's spacious office. As they passed Victor Jennings' office, which was adjacent to April's, Venice glanced inside. Seated behind a huge mahogany desk overflowing with paper was a tall, thin man staring quizzically at his computer screen. His complexion bore traces of many a battle fought with, and lost to, acne in his younger years. He certainly *looked* harmless, Venice thought. But Corinne's words came back to her in a flash: *Don't trust him, Venice. Not for a second.*

Inside April's office, Venice was ordered to sit. She did so as April slammed the door shut behind them.

Venice quickly scanned the office. Nothing out of the ordinary: some filing cabinets, a computer with a large flat-screen monitor, some withered plants, and a desk calendar whose pages hadn't been turned for months. It was the office of a slovenly summer intern, not of a briskly efficient secretary who ran the ship with a tight fist. The large window behind April's desk afforded a nice partial view of Central Park, which was situated about twenty blocks north, but rather than focusing on the view, Venice found herself wishing that the window could be opened to allow some fresh air in. April didn't exactly reek, but her scent, a mixture of sweat, perfume, and deodorant, was far from pleasant.

April sat behind her desk and faced Venice. "Where's your uniform?" she barked.

"Detectives don't wear patrolmen's uniforms, Ms. Lagorda," Venice replied in the tone she sometimes used to tame uncooperative witnesses. "Now, if I can ask you just a few questions. . . ."

"You people *should* wear uniforms. We need more police presence in this city. If the crooks knew cops were around, it would be a deterrent."

"Feel free to write the Commissioner with your thoughts and suggestions," Venice said.

"Maybe I will."

"Now, about the losses. . . ."

"A few wallets and a jacket stolen on Monday and Tuesday. Nothing major until yesterday, when a brand new laptop disappeared from an executive office on the eighteenth floor. This company paid almost two thousand dollars for that computer, and I want it back."

April handed Venice a list she'd compiled the previous evening:

Corinne Jensen — purse with wallet w/ $200 & credit cards

Clive Dudley — leather jacket worth $400

Janet Massou — wallet, $150 & credit cards

Calvin Ziotis — IBM Thinkpad Laptop computer

"Did any of your employees see anyone unfamiliar in the office over the last couple of days?" Venice asked.

"Nobody saw anything. Or at least that's what they say."

"Meaning?"

"There are one or two people who work here that I don't entirely trust."

"You think they might be behind the thefts?"

"I do. They're disgruntled. Instead of appreciating the fact that they have good jobs with a classy publisher, they just go around complaining."

"Do you have any specific evidence? Did you *see* them steal the wallets, the jacket, the purse, or the computer?"

"No. It's just a hunch I have."

"Their names, please?"

"Corinne Jensen and Clive Dudley."

Venice's colleagues downtown were in awe of her poker face; none of them had ever seen her even come close to losing her composure. But Venice was momentarily stunned, and she feared her shock might have registered on her face.

She recovered quickly. "I'm confused. I see those names on this list."

"Do I have to do your job for you, Detective? They're probably in it together. They make themselves into the first victims so nobody suspects them. Then they start their crime spree."

"Any idea what their motivation might be?"

"I told you, they're disgruntled."

"Why?"

"Who knows why? They're two paranoid people with a sense of entitlement. That's all it takes."

"So you think they banded together to steal from their co-workers?"

"They probably need money for their afternoon trysts."

"They're lovers?"

"It's obvious to anybody who looks close enough. They're always in each other's offices and always out to lunch together. Sometimes they take the same days off, too. And her an engaged woman. She should be ashamed of herself. They both should."

Venice pretended to take notes in her little book. "I noticed a camera in the lobby when I walked in, as well as a camera in the hallway on the way to your office. Has anyone looked at the security tapes yet?"

"There's no security tapes."

"Excuse me?"

"Come with me," April ordered. Venice followed April down two hallways, both of which had cameras mounted above them, then up the internal staircase to a corner room labeled "Security Office." April looked around to make sure nobody was in their line of sight, then unlocked the door and motioned Venice in.

April followed and closed the door behind them. Venice looked around, expecting to see TV monitors and other surveillance equipment. Instead, she saw some junky bookcases and an old IBM computer covered by an inch of dust.

"The cameras are fake," April explained. "A lot of companies do it this way. Much cheaper than paying security people or setting up a real security system."

"So the sign in the lobby about the whole floor being under video surveillance is just a grand illusion?"

"It's not an illusion. It accomplishes the same thing as a million-dollar security system. Deterrence."

"Well, it doesn't seem to have deterred anybody this time," Venice said, dryly.

"And that's why it has to be an inside

job," April said, as if explaining a simple concept to a stupid child. "Nobody here knows the cameras aren't real, but if someone found out, they'd know they could steal as much as they wanted without getting caught. And even though Corinne and Clive both work on the seventeenth floor, I've seen them up here a lot in the last couple of weeks. They could have broken into this room and found out."

Venice nodded, as if to thank April for her brilliant sleuthing. "I'll talk to them, and to the other people who had things stolen. Do you have an empty office I can use?"

An hour later, after Venice had gone through the motions with Clive and Janet, she asked to speak to Corinne. Fifteen minutes after that, Corinne emerged from the interrogation office, her face white as a sheet. If she'd had any pangs of conscience about the Gang of Four's plot, they'd all been utterly obliterated.

12

The task at hand took Ollie onto the Internet, a place he could happily play for hours, or even days, at a time.

A few simple Google searches turned up several decent photos of Victor Jennings. Victor appeared in some carefully posed "candid" shots on the Clarendon & Shaw Website, and his picture had been snapped every time he'd made a speech to the American Booksellers Association, usually on such topics as "Ethics in Publishing" or "Pride in Your Employees." Ollie even found Victor's personal Website, on which the Jennings family proudly posted pictures of their four odd-looking children and snapshots from vacations on Nantucket and Martha's Vineyard, featuring Victor in preppy-looking clothes and boat shoes. Ollie copied all the photos onto his hard drive.

But his luck was short-lived. More than three hours of continuous searching yielded not even a single picture of April Lagorda.

His final stop was the Website of a well-known publisher of romance novels. Ollie downloaded the covers of dozens of best-sellers with titles like *Inherit the Sun, Love on the Mayflower, Love's Tender Kiss,* and *Low Tide in Jamaica.* The artwork on all the covers looked as if it had been conceived by the same romantic mastermind: an exotic locale in the background, and in the foreground a scantily clad muscular man with his arms around the waist or shoulders of a raven-haired beauty in tight, ripped clothing.

Do real people really look like that? Ollie wondered as he looked down at his very small, but growing, pot belly. Maybe he should get to the gym more often. . . .

13

Friday evening's dinner took place at Chez Corinne and Ollie. The week had gone more or less according to plan, with only one or two snags.

The best news, they all agreed, was the complete lack of camera surveillance in the Clarendon & Shaw offices. Uncovering this information had been the main purpose of Venice's visit. Corinne had felt pretty sure the cameras were phony, but they'd needed to make sure. They'd also needed to know whether any special security measures were in place for April and Victor's respective offices. The empty "Security Room" had proved there were not.

All of this meant they could sneak in after hours and nobody would be the wiser. Of course, Corinne would have to "sign in" in the lobby, but it wasn't as if the weekend guards (or even the weekday guards) cared about who entered the building. As long as you flashed your employee ID and used your key card to access the elevator, they assumed you had a right to be there and barely looked up from their cell phones or magazines. And it wasn't as if she was going to sign her real name in the lobby's guest registry. . . .

The fly in the ointment was April's complete lack of Web presence. So conversation fell to brainstorming how to get at least one or two decent photos of the camera-shy secretary. Ollie joked that he wouldn't lend his digital camera to the project for fear of its lens cracking when focused on April.

"Leave this to me," Venice said confidently.

14

On Monday, the Clarendon & Shaw receptionist buzzed April. "Detective Calderon is here to see you."

"Sorry to bother you," Venice said breezily, once she was sitting in April's office. "I need. . . ."

"Did you find the computer yet?"

"Not yet."

April rolled her eyes, as if to comment on the incompetence of the New York City police force.

"As I was starting to say," Venice continued patiently, "I need to take some pictures of the various scenes of theft for the guys in forensics." TV shows always seemed to imply that Forensics could solve any crime just by looking at some pictures and putting a few drops of liquid under a microscope, and Venice hoped April bought into the easy view of crime solving promulgated by *CSI: Miami* and its various permutations.

But April was skeptical. "The guys in forensics? How are they going to figure anything out from pictures? You should be fingerprinting people. That's how you'll find your man. And woman."

"Ms. Lagorda, I don't think you understand how sensitive the issue of fingerprinting is. Are you willing to accuse Ms. Jensen and Mr. Dudley openly? If so, I'll bring them in for printing right now. But if we find the computer and the prints don't match up, the two of them will have very good grounds to sue Clarendon & Shaw — and you — for character defamation."

The word *sue* was a magic pixie dust that obliterated April's righteous desire to point an accusing finger. "No, I don't want any trouble for the company. Go ahead, take your pictures."

"I'll need you to bring me to the various locations, please."

So Venice followed as April brought her first to Corinne's office, then to Clive's, Janet's, and Cal's. In each location, Venice tried to get April into the camera's lens, but each time Venice tried to snap a photo, April ducked quickly out of sight. April, it seemed, had been dodging cameras all her life and had become expert in the skill.

An hour later, after carefully looking

through the dozens of pics snapped on the digital camera, a frustrated Venice called Ian. She gave him the news: She'd managed to get portions of April's legs, arms, and ample bosom, but not a single shot of her face.

"Plan B," Ian said.

15

Twenty minutes later, Ian was riding the L train to Williamsburg, Brooklyn, where April lived alone in a one-bedroom condominium in a five-story building. Corinne had gotten April's address from the guys in the mailroom, who distributed the paychecks every two weeks.

During the Gang of Four's last caper, the doormen they'd encountered had proven quite uninterested in exerting themselves, which had made it fairly easy to get into the areas to which they needed access. Crossing his fingers as he entered the building, Ian approached a somnolent man sitting behind an open security desk. The man wore a cracked badge with the name "ZOLTAN."

"NYPD," Ian said, flashing a fake badge and ID he'd ordered through the Internet as Venice had looked in the opposite direction. The doorman snapped awake instantly.

"I need your help," Ian said in a friendly

voice. "Can you let me into apartment 5F for a few minutes, and can you keep this between the two of us? If I find what I'm looking for, there's a fifty-dollar Crime Stoppers tip in it for you."

Like so many other immigrant doormen in New York apartment buildings, Zoltan had an innate fear of the police and little knowledge of search-warrant laws. He disappeared for a minute, came back with a key, and led Ian up to April's apartment. He opened the door, gave Ian the key, and returned to the lobby.

Ian was shocked by the apartment. He and Venice had lavished attention on every square inch of their new home, making it as perfect, inviting, and warm as they could. But April lived in squalor. Dirty clothes were strewn about the floor; newspapers were tied in bundles and stacked six feet high. The linoleum on the kitchen floor looked as if it hadn't been washed in twenty years. The bed was unmade, and the whole apartment smelled dank.

Any normal woman would have at least one or two photos of herself, her friends, and her family somewhere in her home — whether on the refrigerator, on a night table, hanging on a wall, or stuffed into a photo album. But the apartment contained no photos anywhere. No snapshots on the mirror, no pictures in frames, and no photo albums on the crowded bookshelves.

Ian locked the door behind him and returned to the lobby, where he thanked the doorman and handed him two twenties and a ten to ensure his silence. That hurt, a little. Their budget was much tighter on this project than it had been on the Andrew Weisch project. There, they were attempting to recover their principal plus expenses, but here the payoff was nothing more than justice.

On the way out of the building, a thought struck Ian. He returned to the doorman, pointed to the security camera in the lobby, and asked to see the security tapes.

"Camera is phony," Zoltan said in a thick Russian accent.

Aaargh! Ian thought. *Aren't any of the security cameras in this city* real?

16

Venice was sitting in the property manager's second-floor office at 1600 Avenue of the Americas, fifteen floors below the offices of Clarendon & Shaw.

This was a little tricky. She'd made the appointment in her "official" capacity as NYC Assistant District Attorney.

"I appreciate your help, Mr. Martinez," Venice said, shaking the man's hand and sitting down. Frank Martinez was dressed in a designer suit and wore expensive-looking jewelry on both hands. She couldn't go into detail, she said, but they'd received a tip regarding possible terrorist plans for the neighborhood. There was nothing to panic about, she emphasized, as 1600 was *not* the target. Rather, she needed to install a small electronic eye in a corner office that would point directly at a neighboring build-ing and transmit images back to their control center. The occupant of the office wouldn't even know it was there, and for everyone's peace of mind it was important that this secret remain between Mr. Martinez and A.D.A. Calderon.

Like millions of other New Yorkers, Frank Martinez had lived through 9/11 and was willing to do anything in his power to bring terrorists to justice. "Anything to get those lowlifes," Martinez said with feeling, handing her an electronic key that would grant her access to the seventeenth floor, as well as a silver master key that would unlock any office door at Clarendon & Shaw. "When do you need to go in?"

"Sometime over the weekend. I'll call you with an exact time. You'll be able to get my guys in discreetly, right?"

Martinez folded his arms over his chest. "No problem at all."

17

Most of the Clarendon & Shaw editors worked long hours, with few of them ever leaving before 7 or 8 p.m. In contrast, April began shutting down her computer at 4:58 so that she could be waiting for the elevator at 5:00.

But Corinne, Janet, and Clive had spontaneously decided to have dinner at a trendy new restaurant in Clinton (formerly known as "Hell's Kitchen"), and they knew they'd stand a better chance of getting a table if they got there early. Not a bad cover story, should anyone happen to ask why they were all leaving the office on time.

So, at 5 p.m., the three friends were gathered in the lobby to wait for the elevator. When Corinne saw April rounding the corner, she pushed the down button, knowing there'd be a delay of at least a few minutes before the elevator arrived. There was always the chance that April would choose not to ride in the elevator with them — she didn't like mixing with the rabble — or that the car would be too crowded to fit all of them. If that were the case, they'd agreed that Janet (whom April hated the least) would squeeze onto the elevator with April, and that Corinne and Clive would follow in the next car.

Fortunately, only one person was in the elevator when it stopped at the seventeenth floor — Cal Ziotis. Corinne, Clive, and Janet would normally have stepped aside to let April in first, but this time they filed in before her. The goal was to keep April in front of the elevator so they could steer her in the appropriate direction when they got to the lobby. *This is not going to be easy,* Corinne thought. *April always does the opposite of what you want her to do.*

After 9/11, the building management at 1600 Avenue of the Americas had set up an entry-and-exit system that allowed the security personnel to better monitor incoming and outgoing traffic. The north entrance was used solely to enter the building, and the west entrance was used solely to exit the building. When people entered the building, they were directed clockwise along the upper half of a circle to the elevators. When exiting, they were directed along the lower half of the circle toward the two revolving doors of the western exit. Two sets of non-revolving doors at each point of entry/exit were permanently locked and could be used only by disabled people or by parties with permission to do so, usually delivery people bringing large boxes or furniture into or out of the building.

There was a backup at the revolving doors due to some sort of activity on the sidewalk outside the building. To force April through the proper door, Corinne, Cal, Janet, and Clive arranged themselves diagonally behind her, thus preventing her from moving to the other revolving door unless she were willing to charge through them like a linebacker. April would have been more likely to choose that option within Clarendon & Shaw's offices, but once outside the seventeenth and eighteenth floors, her powers greatly diminished and her attitude adjusted . . . slightly.

Once outside, they saw what all the commotion was about: A newscaster from a local television station, spiffily dressed and coiffed, was conducting "man on the street" interviews with passersby. A cameraman stood behind him taking shots of the crowd while a sound man held a boom mike over the interviewees' heads, just out of the camera's range.

The reporter held a microphone emblazoned with the network's logo: WGOF. Ian had designed the logo the night before and had manufactured it from pressboard onto which he'd carefully painted the station's call letters. "WGOF" had been Ollic's idea: the Gang of Four TV network. The camera and mike were on loan from a company that rents such equipment to corporations for use at sales and stockholder meetings.

Ian stuck the microphone in April's face as soon as she exited the building. Meanwhile, the cameraman — Ian's friend Phinnaeus — zoomed in on her.

"Cyrus Lavelle, WGOF TV. Miss, can you tell us what you think about the mayor's plan to hike the subway fare *another* 50 cents?"

April was momentarily shocked into submission. Her colleagues from Clarendon & Shaw were arranged in a semicircle behind her to prevent her from fleeing the camera, but this arrangement proved unnecessary. April stood her ground and regained her bearings.

"What do I think? What do I *think?* I'll tell you what I think. Policemen walking away with million-dollar pensions. Donald Trump making another billion. And who pays? We do, that's who. Nobody cares about us, the working people of this city, the people who keep it running. The mayor thinks he can get a few more dollars a week out of us, so he's going to do it. He thinks we don't have anything to say about it. But let me tell you this, Bloomberg" — she pointed her finger straight at the camera — "if you raise the subway fare even ONE CENT I will personally lead the charge to get you thrown out of office. That's right, you heard me. Even ONE CENT."

The crowd erupted into cheers and applause.

Having had her say, April pushed her way through the crowd and continued down Sixth Avenue. Ian interviewed a few more pedestrians, none of whom were nearly as passionate or eloquent as April, then he and his friends began packing up their equipment. Next stop was Phinnaeus' audio/video studio, where Ollie awaited.

18

Corinne retrieved her cell phone from her purse and punched in a number. Venice answered on the second ring.

"Worked like a charm," Corinne said.

"She didn't run?" Venice asked.

"Not only did she not run, she planted her feet in the sidewalk and threatened to destroy Bloomberg's political career."

Venice laughed heartily.

"On a totally separate note," Corinne continued, "Ian looked *hot.* He actually looks good as a plastic, smarmy reporter. I've never seen him look so conservative. Or his hair look so flat." Flat hair was indeed a rarity for Ian. As Corinne had witnessed when the four of them had lived together, Ian spent a good twenty minutes each morning spiking his hair into different shapes and peaks to reflect his mood and level of adventurousness.

Venice laughed again. "You think that

get-up was good? Wait til you see the little *ensemble* we've been putting together for the big meeting next week."

19

At Phinnaeus' studio, they hit paydirt. Phinnaeus loaded up the tapes and there in living color, her face taking up the entire screen, was April Lagorda.

Both Ian and Ollie shuddered as Phinnaeus helped them do screen captures of April's face, which Ollie saved in files titled Evil1, Evil2, Devil3, SheDevil4, Beelzebub5, Satana6, Mephistophele7, and so forth.

After thanking Phinnaeus for his help, Ian and Ollie shared a cab back to the house on Leroy Street, where Ian snapped some pictures of himself in reporter garb for use in future work before re-converting himself into the workaday Ian. Ollie booted up his Mac and launched all the programs he would need, including the miraculous Adobe PhotoShop. He broke from his work around 10 p.m. and gathered his friends around the computer to display his handiwork. When Corinne, Venice, and Ian arrived, the screen was temporarily blanked out.

"OK, ready? I gotta warn you, it ain't pretty. Girls, avert your eyes."

Ollie clicked a mouse button. In the blink of an eye the screen was filled with images that no self-respecting romance publisher would ever have chosen for the cover of a trade paperback. The cover of *Love on the High Seas*, for example, featured a long-haired pirate standing behind a servant girl wearing tattered rags, grasping her waist and kissing her neck. Onto the pirate's body Ollie had inexpertly grafted Victor Jennings' face, and onto the servant girl's neck he'd grafted one of the recent photos of April.

With a click of the mouse, Ollie displayed a photo he'd pulled from an upscale travel company's Website. In the original photo, an attractive young couple at a beach resort sat at a restaurant table, piña coladas in front of them as they gazed lovingly at each other. In the doctored photo, the man's face was that of Victor Jennings, and the woman's face was that of April Lagorda. It was obvious to even the untrained eye that heads had been pasted onto bodies not their own — but that was exactly the point. The pictures couldn't look too expert.

On and on the cavalcade of images went. The final dozen or so images were solo portraits of Victor onto which Ollie had pasted hearts, flowers, and other romantic symbols.

"Let's pause to consider the multiple levels of meaning here," Ian suggested, in that artistic way of his. "Some might look at Ollie's romance novel covers and think, 'How grotesque.' But does that imply that love and romance are meant only for the beautiful people? How many of the women who purchase these books look like the original cover model, and how many of them can expect a torrid romance with a man like Fabio? And yet nobody would buy a book where the cover models look like themselves. Are romance novels simply escapism? Or do they perpetuate a cycle of lowered self-esteem by making the average woman think she can never measure up, that love is for beautiful models, not for them?"

"Beats me," Ollie said, not quite knowing how else to respond. Abstract thought was not his strong suit.

20

Corinne knocked lightly on the door of April's office.

"Hi, April. Is Victor going to be available to meet with Gabriel Laurentz today?"

Corinne was playing out the protocol of securing time with Victor. First, you asked April far in advance about Victor's availability. Second, April penciled you in, noting truculently that Victor was a very busy man and that things could change at any minute. Third, the day before your meeting, you sent April an e-mail confirming your request. Finally, the day of the meeting, you went to April's office in person to beg her to have Victor keep his appointment.

April flipped through Victor's calendar. "11 a.m.," she said, without looking up. "You can have him until 11:15."

"That's wonderful, April. Thanks. We're so excited to have Gabriel here."

At 10:45, soon-to-be-bestselling author

Gabriel Laurentz stepped off the elevator and announced his name to the receptionist. Laurentz was an extremely austere looking man: shaved head, Leninesque van dyke, piercing blue eyes, and small rectangular glasses whose black frames complemented his black-and-white patterned shirt and black leather pants. The bad-boy effect was completed with a pair of well-worn Harley Davidson boots and an air of complete scorn for the world and everyone around him.

If he'd been blond, down-to-earth, friendly, and smiling, and if he'd carried himself differently, Gabriel Laurentz could have been mistaken for Ian McTeague.

Corinne met Gabriel in the reception area. He greeted her coolly, shaking her extended hand with obvious reluctance. They disappeared into Corinne's office, shut the door, and emerged a few minutes later. Gabriel followed Corinne down the narrow hallway, under the phony security cameras, to April's office. Corinne raised her eyebrows at April as if to ask, "OK to knock on Victor's door?" April nodded once, then went back to staring at her computer screen.

Corinne rapped on Victor's door lightly.

In his small voice, Victor said, "Come in."

"Morning, Victor," Corinne chirped, brightly. "I'm so pleased to introduce you to Gabriel Laurentz."

Victor mumbled something about how good it was to meet Laurentz, then stood and walked over to his conference table, motioning his two visitors to sit down. Victor was never one to shake hands unless the other man extended his hand first, and because Gabriel made no effort in that direction, no hands were shaken.

"How was your flight?" Victor asked.

"Uneventful," Gabriel responded curtly.

"I'm quite a fan of the Getty," Victor said. "My family and I always visit whenever we're on the West Coast. Simply an amazing building and collection."

Victor had garnered all the information he needed about Laurentz's forthcoming book from the précis Corinne had written to prep Victor for the visit. Victor had been reading the précis when Corinne knocked on his office door.

Death at the Getty
by Gabriel Laurentz

This is the first in a projected new series of literary mysteries by Getty Museum curator and Oxford-educated art historian Gabriel Laurentz. The series will feature Getty curator and single mother Lisette LeBlanc as she navigates the politics of the art world while trying to balance the demands placed on her by her precocious 14-year-old son and her various lovers, who run the gamut from a well-known tenor to a mysterious power broker to whom the élite turn when looking to expand or sell from their private collections.

This first installment finds our heroine mysteriously locked in the Getty one night and unable to leave due to the museum's sophisticated security system. Resigned to her fate, Lisette falls asleep in her office but is awakened by the sound of whispering voices. Investigating, she uncovers a plot to replace several of the museum's key works with well-crafted forgeries. As she digs deeper, she finds that no one can be trusted: not the board of trustees, not the governor of California, not even the President of the United States. When her friends desert her, Lisette takes matters into her own hands as the plot thickens and unravels.

I acquired *Death at the Getty* six years ago, prior to HGSG's acquisition of Clarendon & Shaw. The signing was highly competitive; the agent put the book up for auction and received offers immediately from S&S, Vintage, Penguin, Warner, and FSG. We won because of our reputation for quality and because several of our authors recommended Clarendon so highly.

The original manuscript delivery date was set for more than three years ago, but during that time Laurentz became even busier in the art world and the book languished. I would check in with him every few months and be told that he simply didn't have the time to write. Because the advance is tied to manuscript delivery, I didn't push, and the list has been very full for the last several years anyway. I always figured that if and when the manuscript came, room could be made on the list to accommodate it.

So imagine my surprise when, six months ago, Laurentz contacted me to tell me he'd been on a curatorial tour of the Far East and had spent every free moment during the trip working on the book. He sent me the manuscript, and it was everything it promised to be, and more. Martin was highly impressed and asked if we could get it onto the Spring list. Because it required almost no editing (not that Laurentz would have accepted any editing, anyway), we rushed it through production; it will publish two weeks from Friday.

BOMC and Literary Guild have already taken it, and Selma is working on film rights. Ten-city publicity tour is planned for March–May. I have a complete publicity and marketing plan if you'd like to see it. Laurentz is a *hot property,* and I expect *Death at the Getty* to be one of our most successful books of this, or any, year.

When Laurentz is in town next

week, I plan to gently broach the subject of the second book in the series,
which we're going to want soon. Anything you can do to help in this regard
would be most appreciated.

"You're fortunate to be working with
Corinne," Victor continued as Laurentz
glared at him. "There's not a better editor
in the industry. Have the two of you begun
talking about the next book in the series?"

"You people really are vultures," Laurentz
practically spat. "Do you think I just sit at
the keyboard and spew out chapters? Every
word, every phrase, every simile must be
crafted with the utmost care. My first book
hasn't even been published yet, and you
already want another?"

"Gabriel," Corinne put in gently, "please
understand. The only reason we're asking
about a second book is because we know
how successful the first one is going to be.
I'm sure you can think of artists who you
wish had been more prolific, yes? Artists
with limited output deprive the world of
their talent. As your publisher, it's our job
to make sure that doesn't happen to you.
Think of us the way the Renaissance artists

thought of their patrons."

"Patrons were nothing more than rich philistines who treated artists as their personal slaves."

Corinne was amazed. Though she'd prepped Ian extensively and the two of them had practiced several versions of this conversation, she marveled at how convincingly he played the part of the stuck-up, self-impressed, self-important writer.

Victor jumped to Corinne's aid. Earlier in his career — more than twenty years earlier — he'd published several moderately successful books. He hadn't really done anything important since then — and had risen to become president of Clarendon & Shaw only through a series of mergers and acquisitions in which he played the corporate game exceedingly well — but some of his vestigial editorial training and author-management skills kicked in. "I hope you used that exact line somewhere in the book, Gabriel," Victor said, smoothly, flatteringly. "It's precisely that sort of insight your readers are going to want. And once they get it, they're going to want more. And the only way to give it to them will be through another book."

Laurentz seemed mollified, nodding his head ever so slightly, if not in agreement, then at least not in disagreement.

At that moment, Tara Lipscomb from Publicity stuck her head in the door. "Hi, guys," she said brightly, in the way that only fresh-out-of-college publicity assistants could manage. Corinne inwardly winced; Victor didn't like being referred to as "guy" any more than he enjoyed being called "Vic." Though Clarendon & Shaw had a long history of informality and an almost invisible hierarchy, Corinne always felt that Victor would prefer to be called "Mr. Jennings" by everyone, from the first-year editorial assistants right up through publishers who'd worked with the likes of Stephen King, Danielle Steel, and John Grisham.

"Victor, do you mind?" Corinne asked. "PW wants to do a story about Gabriel, and we're hoping to get some shots of the two of you together."

Victor didn't mind at all; the more photos he saw of himself in *Publishers Weekly,* the happier he was. Laurentz made a few snide comments about the idiocy of the reading public as he moved into position next to Victor. Tara snapped a dozen or so photos, then showed them to everyone on the digital camera's screen. In all the photos, Victor and Gabriel looked stiff and awkward, a testament to Tara's photographic capabilities: She'd captured their essences perfectly.

Corinne looked at her watch. "11:15 already! Victor, thank you so much."

"We're very much looking forward to our continuing relationship," Victor said in the same insincere tone he used with every author he'd ever met. Still, Corinne had to give the man a modicum of credit. Like so many twenty-first century publishing executives, he knew nothing about the books his company published or the people who wrote them, but he *had* read Corinne's memo and done what she'd asked him to do.

Corinne and Gabriel returned to her office, where they sat behind closed doors for half an hour before heading to Restaurant 44 for lunch. At 44, they bumped into several editors from competing houses. Corinne enthusiastically introduced Gabriel as a "close friend of Victor Jennings" and "future best-selling author." Sitting at the table next to them was Alicia Weatherbee, a longtime publisher at Simon & Schuster who'd eaten lunch at 44 every Wednesday for the past five years. Corinne kicked Gabriel under the table, a signal to turn on the charm; and as Gabriel flirted with Alicia, Corinne talked about what a coup it was for Clarendon & Shaw to have signed him up.

"And where did Corinne find you?" Alicia asked Gabriel coquettishly, her tone implying that the only correct answer could be "heaven."

"I'd love to take the credit, Alicia, but he belongs to Victor. The Jennings family supports the Getty Museum pretty heavily, Victor and Gabriel found themselves sitting next to each other at an event. . . ."

"A dreadful event," Gabriel put in with a flourish.

". . . and before any of us knew it, Gabriel was in our offices signing a contract for five books. And wait til you see the first one, Alicia. You're going to die of envy."

"I'm already dying," Alicia said, chewing up Gabriel with her eyes. "When your contract expires, you feel free to call me, Gabriel." She handed him a business card that seemed to have materialized out of thin air, then went back to conversing with her lunch companion, whom she'd completely ignored while she spoke with Gabriel.

Walking down 44th Street after lunch, Corinne said, "That couldn't have gone any better. Alicia's the biggest gossip in the industry. Everyone'll know about you by this time tomorrow."

Back at the office, Corinne and Gabriel continued to meet behind closed doors, pretending to talk about manuscripts (in case anyone was listening) and looking at the .jpeg files of the photos Tara had taken a few hours earlier, which she'd e-mailed to Corinne while she and Ian ate lunch. "Just send them to me when they're ready," Corinne had said to Tara earlier in the day. "You have your hands full. I'll get them to *PW*." No need to involve Tara in their scheme; she was too young and idealistic to spoil with a plot to oust an incompetent ladder-climber and his malicious secretary.

Around 3 p.m., Corinne walked Gabriel to the elevator and thanked him for his time, wishing him all the best for the remainder of his trip to New York. As the elevator door closed, Ian gave Corinne his trademark wink.

21

In the old days, Ollie remembered, it had been incredibly difficult to produce your own photographs. Of course he, like so many other teenage boys, had taken pictures with his Polaroid Instant camera, but the film packs were very expensive and the pictures were never very good. Now, thanks to computer technology, you could buy a digital camera, reasonably priced printer, and good photographic paper, and then produce and print out good-quality pictures to your heart's content. And that's exactly what Ollie was doing.

Just to check his handiwork, Ollie grabbed one at random. *Hmmm, not bad,* he thought, proudly. Only an expert would be able to tell that he'd used PhotoShop to clean up the grainy images of April captured from video stills. Of course, April's oversized head looked a bit odd on the body of those 25-year-old cover models, but that was exactly the point. It had to appear that April had made these pictures herself, and if he'd done too good a job, suspicions might have been raised.

Ollie put all the printouts in a manila envelope and walked up the three flights of stairs to Ian's studio. Ian would work his final magic with his Xacto knife, trimming them professionally and making them look as if they'd been printed by the photo lab at Duane Reade.

Ian flipped through the printouts, looked at his watch, then put the envelope aside.

"How about I finish this up after lunch?" Ian suggested. "White Castle?"

"Lead the way, E."

22

"Mr. Han, my friend, Venice Calderon."

"A pleasure to meet you, Mr. Han." Venice extended her hand to the ancient Chinese man.

"Sit, eat donut," Mr. Han barked, shaking Venice's hand before disappearing into the print shop.

The last time Corinne had visited the shop on Little West 12th Street had been more than two years ago, when Mr. Han had printed a batch of customized magazines for the Gang of Four. Those retouched issues of *Art in America* had been a linchpin in their plot to get their money back from the swindler Andrew Weisch.

"This place is asbestos heaven," Venice said, looking around, seating herself at the rickety table and grabbing a Krispy Kreme.

Mr. Han returned ten minutes later with a box of 50 freshly printed trade paperbacks. He placed the box on the table and Corinne removed the first copies of *Death at the Getty* to see the light of day. Ian had done a beautiful job designing the cover, a job he'd relished because he'd never done a book's cover design before. Ollie had used a page make-up program called Quark XPress to typeset the entire manuscript from scratch.

Of course, the most important page of the book was the last page. Corinne turned to page 356 to make sure the acknowledgments page was there; and indeed it was.

"These look great, Mr. Han," Corinne said. "Thank you so much."

"No. Thank you. I call Mr. Cal Ziotis next week."

In plotting to get their money back from Weisch, they'd had to invest plenty of their own money, and they'd done so willingly, expecting they'd get it all back when their plot succeeded. This was a slightly different situation, though; printing more than four dozen books was a very expensive operation that the Gang of Four wasn't really willing to pay for, especially since there would be no monetary payoff from this operation.

But the copies of *Death at the Getty* were an essential part of the plan, so they'd had to find a way to make it work. That's where Cal Ziotis came in. As Director of Production and Manufacturing, he was responsible for getting all of Clarendon & Shaw's books printed and bound. He would never have given work to a small operation like Mr. Han's, whose shop's pricing structure couldn't compete with that of the larger operations like R.R. Donnelly. But Cal had called Mr. Han and said he was looking for a local vendor to provide support on an ad hoc basis, and he'd asked Mr. Han if he'd be willing to do a sample job for them. An experienced businessman, Mr. Han looked on the job as an investment in building a relationship with Clarendon & Shaw, one that could lead to substantial work (and profit) further down the road.

Corinne and Cal had discussed the situation. She didn't want to steal free printing from Mr. Han, whom she liked a great deal. Cal had told her not to worry about it; he'd be sure to send some jobs Mr. Han's way over the next couple of months. He was, after all, the Director of Production and Manufacturing, and no one was going to question his decision.

"That donut only made me hungrier," Venice said, helping Corinne pack the books into two large satchels they'd brought in which to haul the books home. "How about some lunch?"

"Let's. I've been so good lately, I could

really use something tasty and fattening."

"Do we dare?"

"What are you thinking, Miss Calderon?"

"A certain Castle colored White has a certain appeal to it. . . ."

"I wonder if the guys will be there?"

23

"Ms. Lagorda, it's Detective Calderon. I have good news. We've recovered the computer stolen from your offices."

April was not one to flirt with any of the more positive emotions, but she let out a grunt of unexpected pleasure despite herself.

"It showed up at a pawn shop in SoHo," Venice continued. "It matches the serial number you gave us."

"Did you get the thief?"

"Unfortunately, pawn shop owners are not always overly careful in that regard. He says he bought it from a guy he'd never seen before."

"Why don't you show him a picture of Clive Dudley? I bet it was him."

"There are certain constitutional issues with that course of action."

April made a noise of indignation.

"Anyway," Venice continued, "my partner

and I will be passing your building in about half an hour. I'll have the computer with me. I have a busy day, so I'd appreciate it if you could meet me in the lobby instead of my having to come all the way up to your offices."

April wasn't accustomed to going out of her way to help anyone, but she knew how the police worked — she wouldn't have been surprised if the laptop managed to "disappear" again en route to the Clarendon & Shaw offices.

"Fine, I'll meet you in the lobby."

"OK, it's 1:30 now . . . let's say 2 p.m.? I'll call you when I'm a few blocks from your building."

At 1:55 Corinne's phone rang. Corinne answered it, then called Janet. At 1:56, Janet moved into position, waiting for April to pass her office on the way to the elevator. At 1:58, April's phone rang, and at 1:59 April and Janet were waiting for the elevator. Janet's hands were in her pockets, her index fingers poised to hit the "call" button to dial the numbers she'd punched into two separate cell phones. If anything went wrong — if April didn't get on the elevator, or if she didn't get off on the ground floor, or anything else — she'd hit the "call" button on the phone in her right pocket. Corinne's cell phone would ring, and the mission would be temporarily aborted. If everything went according to plan, Janet would hit the call button of the cell phone in her left pocket. She'd borrowed this cell phone from Cal Ziotis, and the number waiting to be called belonged to Ollie's cell phone, which was sitting on Corinne's desk next to her own cell phone.

The elevator arrived. April entered, followed by Janet. When the elevator reached the ground floor, April exited and followed the traffic-flow pattern set up by building security. They rounded the corner, and standing there at the security desk was Venice holding a laptop computer.

Janet hit the call button of the phone in her left pocket as she walked out of the building. A fraction of a section later, Corinne's cell phone rang.

Corinne had been waiting at the door of her office, two advance copies of *Death at the Getty* in one hand and a computer diskette in the other hand. She strode quickly down the hall to April's office, passing Victor Jennings' office on the way. She needed an excuse if she was found in April's office, and the advance copies of *Death at the Getty* were a perfect cover story. Upon publication of a new book, each editor brought April two copies, one for Victor's private collection in his office, the other to be archived in the company's library. If she were caught behind April's desk, she'd say she was looking for a pen to write April a note.

Victor was in his office but was, as always, staring intently into his computer screen and oblivious to his surroundings. Corinne entered April's office, gently pushed the door closed, stuck the diskette into the A drive of April's computer, then followed the directions Ollie had given her for executing the program. The fifteen seconds it took for the program to install on April's machine were the longest fifteen seconds of Corinne's life. She breathed a sigh of relief when the long-awaited box finally appeared:

Installation Complete.

She popped the diskette out of the drive, left the two copies of *Death at the Getty* in the large IN box on April's desk, then took the long way back to her office to avoid walking past Victor's office again.

Once in her office, she shut the door and sat down at her desk, her heart pounding like mad and her body shaking a little.

Ten minutes later, her phone rang. It was

Venice. "Mission accomplished here. How about there?"

"Here too," Corinne said.

24

Just as Corinne was about to leave for the day, an e-mail blipped in from Tara in Publicity. "Check out the Website," the e-mail said. "The *Death at the Getty* page is ready."

Corinne launched her browser, which was set to the Clarendon & Shaw homepage. A large banner took up the top half of the screen real estate. "Just published! *Death at the Getty,* by Gabriel Laurentz. For details, CLICK HERE."

Corinne clicked on the link and was taken to a splashy page for the book. Prominently featured were the biography of Gabriel Laurentz — which, strangely enough, did not mention anything about his being a curator at the Getty — as well as two of the photos of Gabriel and Victor buddying it up.

The Web people had done a nice job on short notice. Like Tara, they had no idea that their services were being used in pursuit of a greater good; they'd simply responded to Corinne's request for new materials on the Website with their usual aplomb. Book schedules were always changing; they were used to doing things on the fly.

Corinne shut down her computer, turned off her desk light, and went home. It wouldn't be long now.

25

There was a chance that some of her fellow editors would be working at ten p.m. on a Saturday, but only a small one. She had her excuse ready: "Left my cell phone here yesterday!"

When she and Ollie arrived at the building, Corinne used her electronic key to enter the front door, then flashed her ID at the night security guard, who pointed to the registration book on a stand in the center of the lobby. Corinne signed in as "Emma Peel." Directly below, Ollie signed his name: John Steed. Both indicated that they were visiting the twelfth floor, not the seventeenth.

The Clarendon & Shaw offices were dark and quiet. After walking casually around both the seventeenth and eighteenth floors, they felt confident they were alone.

Reaching into her pocket, Corinne pulled out the master office key that Venice had secured from Frank Martinez. Within seconds, Ollie was seated at April's chair, booting up her computer. In the meantime, Corinne went to her office and typed an e-mail to Victor Jennings, then hit "send."

When prompted to enter a password on April's computer, Ollie clicked several keys that allowed him to access the program that Corinne had installed a few days previously. That program, KEY CAPTURE, is closely guarded by IT directors because it offers so much potential for misuse. When installed on a machine, it captures every individual keystroke from the minute the computer is turned on until the minute it is turned off — thus making it easy not only to keep track of an employee's work, but also to decipher his or her passwords. Ollie'd had to sneak into his supervisor's private archives to borrow the program; he'd done so by arranging a lunch for the department at a local restaurant, then leaving early due to "stomach problems."

April's password, it turned out, was TUNAFISH.

"Well, looky here," Ollie said when Corinne rejoined him in April's office. "Looks like our friend is quite the little spy."

By tracing April's daily routine, Ollie was able to figure out exactly what April did to earn her salary. She started the day by checking her e-mail, then logging on to a few soap opera Websites and newsgroups, to which she posted prodigiously under the name "NewYorkLady." This was followed by an hour or two of "spying" on individual employees, accessing their e-mail and desktops through a program that allows company executives and IT specialists to do exactly that. April, it seemed, routinely read through both the incoming and outgoing e-mail of just about everyone in the office. For much of the afternoon, April played solitaire or other online games, then usually ended the day by spying on a few more Clarendon & Shaw workers.

"Well, here goes nothing," Ollie said, retrieving some CD-ROMs from a small case he'd smuggled into the building. He opened April's Outlook e-mail account, then watched as Corinne prepared a sequence of e-mails from April to various Internet bulletin boards and newsgroups. The entire **Clarendon & Shaw Employees** mailing list — minus April and Victor, of course — was "accidentally" cc'ed on each e-mail. Ollie attached a photograph from the CD-ROM to each e-mail, instructing Outlook to send the first e-mail at 10 a.m. on Monday, the second at 10:30, and the third at 11:00.

Corinne knew that April somehow had access to Victor's e-mail account and that Victor seldom read his own e-mail. Any time she wrote an e-mail to Victor, she got a response directly from April, never from Victor himself. Ollie — who knew Outlook like the back of his hand — easily figured out how to access Victor's e-mail from April's computer. He opened Victor's account, then once again ceded the chair to Corinne, who first deleted the e-mail she'd sent to Victor five minutes earlier and then typed two e-mails from Victor to "Corinne Jensen." Ollie set the timing on the e-mails so that the first would be delivered on Monday morning, the second on Tuesday afternoon.

As Ollie uninstalled KEY CAPTURE from April's machine, Corinne went to her office to retrieve both a manila folder and a hanging folder. She took a chewed-up pen from April's pencil cup and wrote "Victor" on the tab. Then she took the photos that Ollie had printed out and Ian had trimmed, and dumped them into the manila folder. She then pulled the key to April's filing cabinet from underneath the spider plant where it was "hidden," unlocked the cabinet, and squeezed the hanging folder amongst all the other junk crammed into the cabinet. She relocked the filing cabinet and returned the key to its hiding place as Ollie powered down April's machine.

They were out of the building by 10:45 p.m. By 11:05, they were pre-celebrating at Zanzibar in Hell's Kitchen, where Venice and Ian were already enjoying cocktails.

26

On Monday morning, Frank Martinez received a small package. Inside were the master office key and electronic key card he'd given to A.D.A. Calderon, along with a note.

Dear Mr. Martinez:
Thank you for your assistance. I'm returning your keys herewith. It turns out the information we received was inaccurate, which I suppose we should be thankful for. I'd appreciate your continued discretion in this matter.

Sincerely,
Venice Calderon

Martinez put the keys back into the storage cabinet and didn't give the matter a second thought.

27

Corinne was sitting at her desk on Monday morning, trying to read a manuscript, when a beep from her computer alerted her that it was 10 a.m. She toggled from Microsoft Word to Microsoft Outlook and sure enough, there was the e-mail from Victor that she'd typed on Saturday night. There was also an e-mail from April Lagorda. With a cat-that-ate-the-canary smile on her face, she clicked open Victor's e-mail, then April's.

To: Listserv@MyBossIsHot.com
cc: Clarendon & Shaw Employees
Fr: April Lagorda
   <alagorda@clarendonshaw.com>
Re: the latest
hello ladies —
here's a little something for y'all to envy.
flew to hawaii with v.j. over the weekend
. . . strolled on the beach and picked up

seashells, then dinner at a very romantic place on the ocean . . . the evening ended with us making sweet love at one of the most exclussive hotels in Honnolulu . . . here's a pic of us for all u busy bodies! more soon - and eat your hearts out

amber vixen

Embedded in the e-mail the "romantic couple at dinner with piña coladas" photo Ollie had created.

Corinne didn't dare leave her office until after 10:30, when the second e-mail arrived.

To: Listserv@MyBossIsHot.com
cc: Clarendon & Shaw Employees
Fr: April Lagorda <alagorda@clarendon shaw.com>
Re: so you want more
ladies, ladies –
alright, you have to stop pestering me. YES: it was as romantic as it looks, we had wine and conversation and he told me he loved me for the first time! i don't care what anyone says, theres lots of benefits to being the other woman . . . u get your fun, u get your man at his best, and i now have lots of beautifull jewlery i never had before.

so here is another, and maybe i will

share more just to show all u ladies what u r missing. . . .

amber vixen

Embedded in this e-mail was another piece of Ollie's handiwork, a photo of "Victor" and "April" strolling hand in hand on the beaches of Waikiki.

As Corinne had hoped, she passed several closed doors on the way to the coffee room. This was a good sign that people were locked inside, excitedly gossiping. There was plenty of gossip to be had in the coffee room, too, where three editors were giggling nervously as they expressed their complete lack of surprise at the situation. Everyone knew April was in love with Victor, said Meryn, an editor who'd been working at Clarendon for nearly a decade. Corinne listened as a new editor named Gian — one of the more tech-savvy guys on the editorial staff — hypothesized about exactly what had happened.

"I went to MyBossIsHot.com to check it out. It's a Website for secretaries who are secretly in love with their bosses, or are carrying on affairs with their bosses. I looked on the site archive, and there must be two dozen postings from 'Amber Vixen' about her exploits with 'V.J.' " He framed both names with air quotes.

Corinne just nodded, silently congratulating Ollie on having done that part of the job so well. Over the past few weeks, he'd regularly posted notes written by Corinne under the pseudonym "Amber Vixen" to the MBIH.com listserv, using a free Hotmail e-mail account he'd set up.

"But how did we ending up getting copies of those e-mails?" Corinne dared to ask. "You'd think she'd be a little more careful."

"There must be a virus that's copying private e-mails and sending them to the mailing lists," Gian said. "Or she just did it by accident. She might have thought she was in her private e-mail account, and instead she was in her company e-mail. Or something like that."

"Wait till Human Resources gets wind of this," said Meryn.

"Never mind *that*," Gian replied. "Wait til *Mrs. Victor Jennings* hears about it."

Coffee in hand, Corinne returned to her office, noticing along the way that even more office doors were closed.

At 11 a.m., the third e-mail hit. This one outlined "Amber Vixen's" burgeoning career as a romance novelist and included the cover art for the first three of her books, which her publisher was about to release.

The text of that e-mail promised even more photos in the coming days, all of which, Amber Vixen said, she had stored in a safe place in her filing cabinet at work.

Around noon, the quiet started to get to Corinne. She couldn't concentrate on anything, and she was too paranoid to call Ollie, Venice, or Ian. To work off some of her nervous energy, she strolled past Victor and April's offices. April wasn't in her office, and Victor's door was closed.

Corinne was rounding the corner on her way to the ladies' room when she nearly collided with Karla Freschetti, the Director of Human Resources. Karla almost never left her office at HGSG's corporate headquarters on West 57th Street.

"Hi, Karla," Corinne said, pleasantly. She and Karla were on good terms, having spent many an hour chatting at corporate events and book parties. "What brings you here?"

As H.R. people tend to do when trouble is afoot, Karla became very close-lipped. "Meeting with Victor," she said evasively, slipping past Corinne as she strode purposefully toward Victor's office.

Corinne couldn't take it any more. She had to get out. She went to her office, retrieved her purse, and went to lunch. She wanted nothing more than to talk with Janet, Clive, and Cal, but they'd all agreed to have no contact the entire day. So Corinne fled the building and walked up Avenue of the Americas to Central Park, stopping for a Diet Coke and a copy of *The New Yorker* along the way. She found a bench in the park, popped open the soda, and got engrossed in a new story by Jonathan Franzen, whom she liked as a writer but not as a person. Finishing the story, she looked at her watch and realized she'd been gone nearly two hours.

Back at Clarendon & Shaw, office doors were still shut. She couldn't take it any more. Rather than going directly to her office, she knocked on Janet's door. Surely nobody would think there was anything amiss about that — she and Janet were *friends,* after all.

"Come in," Janet said airily.

Corinne popped her head in the door. "Hey . . ."

Janet motioned for Corinne not to say anything. Then she started scribbling furiously on her notepad. She held up the notepad for Corinne to read:

WALK PAST APRIL'S OFFICE.

Corinne nodded and backed out of Janet's office. She casually strolled down the hallway, took a right, then a left, and found herself passing the offices of her nemeses.

April's office was dark. The door was locked. Her nameplate was gone.

Back in her office, Corinne picked up her cell phone and called Ollie. Then she called Venice, and then Ian. She said the same thing to all three of them:

"One down, one to go."

28

As word of April's termination spread, the offices of Clarendon & Shaw experienced a jubilation they hadn't felt since the days before Victor and April arrived two years earlier. All the celebrating went on behind closed doors, of course. Everyone knew how "close" Victor and April were, and celebrating April's demise too openly would not have stood anyone in good stead with Mr. Jennings.

On Tuesday afternoon, the second e-mail from Victor blipped into Corinne's e-mail box. She opened it and quickly forwarded it according to plan, just as she'd done with Victor's first e-mail from the day before.

To her surprise, she found herself sharing the elevator with Victor at the end of the day. The man looked downtrodden.

"You doing OK, Victor?" Corinne asked him, kindly, pushing the "L" button.

Victor sighed. "It's been a rough couple

of days, Corinne."

Corinne resisted the temptation to reach out and pat Victor's shoulder. Instead, she said, "Oh, try not to worry, Victor. I'm sure things will get better."

29

The following morning, Corinne received an angry phone call from Kaz Kazinski, an agent with whom she'd worked closely for several years.

"I'll be there in an hour. Tell Vic I expect to see him."

"Kaz, I'm not sure he's available. He doesn't have an assistant right now. . . ."

"Like I said, I'll be there in an hour. If he doesn't have time to see me, tell him I'll be back tomorrow with enough lawyers to eat up Clarendon & Shaw's profits for the next three decades." He hung up the phone.

Not quite knowing what to do, Corinne went to Victor's office and stuck her head in the door.

"Victor, excuse me, I hate to bother you, but I think we may have an urgent situation."

Victor looked up from his computer screen as if to say: *Oh, no. What now?*

"I just got an irate phone call from Kaz Kazinksi. He says he needs to see you and that he'll be here in an hour. He's threatening legal action."

"Legal action? Over what?"

"I don't know. But he sounded like he meant business."

Victor sighed loudly. In the old days, publishers took great pride in publishing controversial books that stirred the pot and muddied the waters. But that was in the good old twentieth century. In the twenty-first, the multinational corporations that own the publishers live in fear of being sued and gladly throw authors or employees to the wolves to avoid costly litigation.

"I'll ask Zena at reception to bring him to my office when he gets here, and then I'll bring him to see you, OK?" Corinne said gently, doing her best to feign concern for Victor and his predicament.

Kaz arrived in high dudgeon forty-five minutes later.

"What's this all about, Kaz?" Corinne asked as they sat in her office.

"What's this all about? How about theft of intellectual property, pure and simple?"

"Kaz, what are you talking about?"

"Corinne, we've always gotten along. I know you don't have anything to do with

321

this. Let's go see Vic."

Two minutes later, the three of them were sitting at Victor's conference table.

"Kaz," Victor began in his most conciliatory voice. "What's all this talk about lawyers and suing?"

"I've known you a long time, Vic," Kaz said, his anger barely controlled. "You've done some sleazy things in your time, but this is the *worst*. How could you think I wouldn't find out? Or did you just think you could get a group of lawyers together and bully me?"

"You're one to talk about sleazy, Kaz. We haven't sold a single copy of *Troubled Love* since that article in the *Clarion*."

"Yeah, but you sold a million copies before that, and I didn't hear you complaining."

"How about sparing me the hypocrisy and getting to the point, Kaz?"

Kaz reached into the satchel he'd been carrying. With one hand he pulled out a copy of *Death at the Getty*. He threw it on the conference table. Then, with the same hand, he pulled out a large manuscript held together by rubber bands. The title page read:

An Artful Way to Die

a novel
by Willis Grant

Kaz threw the manuscript on the table in front of Victor. "Go ahead, Vic. Compare them."

Victor flipped open to the first page of *Death at the Getty,* then turned to the first page of the manuscript. The published book and the manuscript were exactly the same, word for word.

"Corinne, what's going on here?"

Corinne, who'd been looking at the manuscript and published book at the same time as Victor, extended her hands and shook her head as if to say, *I have no idea.*

"I'll tell you what's going on, Vic," Kaz said. "Tell me if this sequence of events sounds familiar, OK? Willis Grant sends you his manuscript a year ago, and you send him a rejection letter." Kaz pulled another document out of his satchel: a rejection letter dated a year earlier and signed by Victor. "You don't feel like taking a chance on an unknown writer, because you're a coward like every other publisher in this town. Then you meet Gabriel Laurentz and decide that Grant's book could fly if it were written by a curator at the Getty instead of a poor NYU art history student. And *voilà!* A year later, the book that I took on six months ago comes out as *Death at the Getty,* 'written' by Getty curator Gabriel Laurentz."

"This is insane," Victor replied. "I never saw that manuscript. April must have rejected it for me. Besides, I'm not even Laurentz's editor. Corinne is."

"Then what about all of those buddy pictures of you and Laurentz on the Clarendon Website?"

"Laurentz was here a couple of weeks ago meeting with Corinne. We took a few shots to send to PW."

"I see. Then how do you explain this?"

Kaz grabbed the copy of *Death at the Getty,* turned to the last page of the book, and handed it to Victor. Victor read:

ACKNOWLEDGMENTS

I am indebted to more people than I can possibly acknowledge. For their valuable research assistance I would like to offer my sincere thanks to Betty Larimer, Keisha Williams, Trent Nguyen, and Bailey Powell. For helping to keep my plot on track and my characters believable, I am grateful to the careful eyes of Jennifer Resinski and Larry Watson.

The biggest thanks, however, must go to Victor Jennings of Clarendon & Shaw. From the moment we met at a Getty fund-raising event, Victor has been a trusted friend and advisor. He read every word of the manuscript through successive drafts, taking time from his busy schedule to help me become a better writer. Every one of his suggestions improved this book. Every writer should be fortunate enough to have an editor as dedicated and brilliant as Victor, and it is with admiration and respect that I dedicate *Death at the Getty* to him.

Victor looked even more perplexed. "This is crazy. I met Gabriel Laurentz exactly once. I never read a word of this manuscript."

Corinne grabbed the book and read the acknowledgments. Again she shook her head in confusion.

"Vic, how stupid do you think I am?"

"Calm down, Kaz. There has to be an explanation."

"Yeah, the explanation is that you're a liar and a thief. Well, you're not going to get away with it. You'll be hearing from my lawyers. And maybe I'll call the *Times* and PW, too, and let them know what's going on around here."

"Kaz. . . ."

But Kaz had packed up his papers and walked out the door.

30

Harry Hsin's office was located in corporate headquarters on West 57th. Born and raised in Hong Kong, Harry divided his time according to the season: autumn in the New York office, winter in the Hong Kong office, spring in the London office, and summer in the Toronto office.

He'd just arrived for the morning when his secretary, who was on the phone, motioned that she needed him. She quickly said good-bye to whomever she was talking to.

"What's up?" Harry asked. When in America, he tended to talk like Americans.

"There's a lot going on at Clarendon, apparently." She ran through the details of the scandal surrounding Victor Jennings' recently terminated secretary, then summarized the communiqué she'd received from the legal department an hour earlier: Kaz Kazinski, a well-known New York literary agent with a slightly tarnished reputation, was suing Clarendon for $150 million on behalf of one of his clients.

Harry listened, taking it all in, asking pointed questions here and there.

". . . but here's the strangest part, Harry," continued the secretary, who was as loyal to Harry as April had been to Victor. "Martin Donovan called me just a few minutes ago to ask if you'd read your e-mail this morning. I said you weren't in yet, so he asked me to have you read his e-mail as soon as possible. I saw it in your e-mailbox, but it's marked confidential so I didn't open it. I didn't even know he'd been let go, did you?"

"Let go? When?"

"Apparently he was fired a month or so ago."

"What? Why didn't Jennings tell me this?"

"I don't know, Harry. But Martin said you'd want to see his e-mail. I have a feeling it might have something to do with the lawsuit."

Harry Hsin nodded and went into his office. Thanks to his able secretary, who always booted up his computer first thing in the morning, he was able to sit at his desk and access Martin's e-mail with a quick double-click.

To: Harry Hsin <hhsin@hgsg.com>
From: Martin Donovan <MartinDonovan @hotmail.com>
Subject: Urgent
Please treat this as confidential.

Good morning, Harry:

I hope this e-mail finds you well. I've been meaning to write or call since I was let go from Clarendon last month, but I confess I've found myself simply catching up on sleep and reading all those books I never had time to read when I was a publisher. I'd be lying if I said I miss Clarendon & Shaw, but I *do* miss our chats and hope we'll stay in touch.

That said, I confess I find myself in a somewhat awkward position. A former colleague of mine from Clarendon — I'm sure you've met her, Corinne Jensen . . . lovely person and fabulous editor — has asked my advice on a situation that's disturbing her greatly. She finds herself in an unsavory ethical dilemma, and she doesn't know how to proceed. She thought I might be able to help.

Before I go any further, let me say that I was as shocked by what Corinne told me as by anything I've seen in my entire career. This is why I'm writing to you. If word of the situation gets out, there could very well be a serious negative impact on HGSG and its stock price. After much thought, I decided you need to know what's going on.

Below I am forwarding a sequence of e-mails I received from Corinne, in which she and Victor correspond regarding the issue. These e-mails speak for themselves, so I'll let them do just that. I've cut and pasted them so that they appear in chronological order.

>>>>To: Victor Jennings
>>>>From: Corinne Jensen
>>>>Subject: Laurentz Title
>>>>Priority: Urgent

Victor: I tried to get in to see you all day yesterday, but April told me you were booked with meetings. So I'm writing to you instead, hoping that we'll be able to talk as soon as you've read this. (It's Saturday right now; I will be in the office first thing Monday morning.)

Kaz Kazinski and I had lunch yesterday (can't stay mad at him forever, given the talent he manages to find), and he was pitching some manuscripts to me. One of them, *An Artful Way to Die,* sounded a lot like the manuscript we're about to publish by Gabriel Laurentz,

Death at the Getty. I told Kaz I'd like to take a look, so we swung by his office after lunch and I took a copy of the first couple of chapters back to the office with me. Then I tracked down some of the proof of *Death at the Getty* to compare them, and I was shocked by what I saw. Victor, <u>they are the exact same book.</u>

I know how hard you worked on *Death at the Getty* and that it's one of your favorite projects, but I really think we need to postpone the publication until we figure out what's going on. I took the liberty of talking to Cal, and he told me that it's in the warehouse but hasn't begun shipping yet. So it's not too late.

Please give me a call as soon as you can.

Thanks,
Corinne

>>>To: Corinne Jensen
>>>From: Victor Jennings
>>>Subject: Laurentz Title
>>>Priority: Urgent

Corinne, you need to keep your nose out of this. *Death at the Getty* is in for a lot of units, and we need those units to make the third quarter numbers. I'm aware of the issues with the manuscript but decided to move ahead with it anyway. Kazinski's client is a nobody. The book wouldn't sell with his name on it, but it'll sell plenty with Laurentz's. So just let this go and I'll deal with it.

>>To: Victor Jennings
>>From: Corinne Jensen
>>Subject: Laurentz Title
>>Priority: Urgent
  Victor:
  I received your e-mail and I have to admit that I was quite surprised by it. There are serious ethical issues involved here. At the last annual meeting, Harry Hsin talked about how HGSG has always prided itself on being both profitable and socially responsible at the same time, and he encouraged us to maintain the highest standards in that regard. I can't help but think that we are flying in the face of our parent company's mantra with this situation, and I'm very concerned about the fallout for Clarendon & Shaw if word of this gets out, which it almost certainly will.
  Please reconsider.

                                    Corinne

>To: Corinne Jensen
>From: Victor Jennings
>Subject: Laurentz Title
>Priority: Urgent

Corinne, I've told you to keep your nose out of this, and I mean it. We already have back orders for more than 50,000 copies of the Laurentz book, and we need the revenue. It's revenue that pays your salary, just in case you haven't yet figured out how this business works.

As for Harry Hsin and his blather about ethical standards, it's all nonsense. The HGSG annual report contains more fiction than any novel we publish, and I could tell you a few stories about Harry that would show him up for the hypocrite he is.

This is the last I expect to hear from you on this matter. Case closed.

Harry, I'm sorry to have to send you such offensive e-mails, and I fear that you'll think my contacting you solely an exercise in sour grapes after my dismissal. While it's true that I do hold a certain amount of animosity toward Victor, that isn't what's motivating me here. I worked at Clarendon & Shaw for more than 35 years, and during those years we were a proud, respected, *respectable* publisher. It pains me to see what's becoming of the company on Victor's watch, and I thought you should be aware of the example he is setting.

Kind regards,
Martin

Harry Hsin hadn't become the CEO of a global corporation by overreacting. It was quite possible that Martin Donovan, whom he liked very much, had become a vindictive liar whose chief goal in life was to destroy Victor Jennings. A few discreet queries would answer all of Harry's questions.

He picked up the phone and called his Chief Information Officer. "Get me copies of any e-mails that Victor Jennings sent to Corinne Jensen in the last month," he ordered. Then he called the Director of Contracts and asked that a .pdf file of the Laurentz contract for *Death at the Getty* be e-mailed to him immediately.

Within an hour, the IT department confirmed that Victor had sent Corinne two e-mails in the last month and sent copies of those e-mails to Harry. They exactly matched those in Martin's e-mail. Fifteen minutes later, a copy of the Laurentz contract showed up in Harry's e-mailbox. Harry page-forwarded to the last page of the contract, which was signed by Gabriel Laurentz, Author and Victor Jennings, President.

Blather about ethical standards? Fiction-filled annual report? Stories about the CEO and his hypocrisy? Surely this was not the way the president of HGSG's major publishing unit should be talking.

His secretary buzzed him. The lawyers wanted to talk to him, she said. Apparently they'd had a call from Kaz Kazinski, who also wanted to talk to Harry Hsin privately.

"Get him on the phone," Harry said.

31

The Clarendon & Shaw staffers who arrived first thing Monday morning didn't notice anything amiss. They unlocked their offices, turned on their computers, and got their coffee, just as they did every other Monday.

It was Jeremy, the mailroom guy, who first noticed.

"Hey," he asked Clive. "What happened to Victor's nameplate? It's gone."

Clive rushed to Victor's office, which was locked and dark. The nameplate was indeed gone, perhaps tossed into the trash incinerator next to April's.

32

An e-mail from Harry Hsin's office arrived around 11 a.m. It was direct and to the point.

Dear Colleagues:

I regret to announce that Victor Jennings has left us to pursue other interests. I'm sure you will all join me in thanking Victor for his many contributions to Clarendon & Shaw over the past two years.

I'll be visiting your offices this afternoon to talk about some changes we'll be making in the organization. Please join me in the eighteenth floor conference room at 2 p.m. Coffee and donuts will be provided.

I look forward to seeing all of you.

Sincerely,
Harry Hsin

Little work was done between the hours of 11 and 2, as staffers celebrated by popping open hastily-bought bottles of champagne. At 2 p.m., the conference room was full to bursting when Harry Hsin walked in.

As always, Harry was calm and charismatic. He thanked everyone for coming and then got down to business.

"As you all know, Victor has left the company. It's not worth going into the details, but we all know how gossipy this industry is, and I'm sure most of you already know everything there is to know anyway." Karla Freschetti, standing off to Harry's side, grimaced with disapproval at Harry's levity.

"On a serious note, though, there *is* something I'd like to talk with all of you about: money. Of course HGSG wants Clarendon & Shaw to earn a lot of money. That's why we're in business — to make money. And making money isn't a bad thing, especially when it comes from doing what we love and doing it well. When we publish good books, we make money while helping people learn or escape or grow. And with that money, we can invest in young writers with fresh voices and keep this great company strong. But money isn't the only thing we care about. We care about quality, too, and about dealing fairly and ethically with our authors and colleagues. At the end of any business day, we want to hold our heads high and say we did the right thing.

"I'd guess that everyone in this room went into this business because you love books. Am I right? Well, I love books, too. So does the board of directors. We've always considered Clarendon & Shaw our classiest company, the one we're proudest of. Everyone in this room does this company proud, and I feel honored to be here among you. So, thank you all."

There was a moment of hushed silence in the room as the employees of Clarendon & Shaw took in Harry Hsin's message. They weren't used to compliments; none of them had ever heard a single word of appreciation from Victor Jennings.

"That said," Harry Hsin continued, "I feel that the person who leads this company needs to be completely in sync with Clarendon's proud heritage and have a plan for its future. And I think everyone will agree that there's one man who's perfect for the job. So, without further ado, let me introduce the new president of Clarendon & Shaw."

On cue, the door opened and Martin Donovan walked in.

33

Corinne and her partners in justice would have loved nothing more than to relax the entire weekend, but alas — there was entertaining to be done. It had been a busy week, but it was time to celebrate another plot flawlessly executed by the Gang of Four.

The guests started arriving at Corinne and Ollie's apartment around 8 p.m. on Saturday. Martin and Jeanne were the first to arrive. Behind them two delivery guys lugged in expensive caviar, canapés, and bottles of wine from Martin's extensive collection. Venice and Ian arrived a few minutes later, and the six friends uncorked a fine Italian burgundy to enjoy before the remainder of the guests arrived.

"A toast," said Martin, raising his glass. "To Corinne, for her beauty and brilliance. To Oliver, for his computer skills. To Venice, for her sense of justice and inside contacts. And to Ian, master artist, journalist, novelist, museum curator, and forger."

It wasn't as easy as it looked, Ian thought. He'd had to practice Victor's signature for days before getting it right. By the time he'd signed Victor's name to the rejection letter to poor Willis Grant and the phony contract for *Death at the Getty,* though, he'd had it down cold.

"Hear, hear," Jeanne said. "To all of you, with my eternal thanks for getting Martin out of my hair and back into the workplace." She reached into her bag and pulled out four small boxes, handing one box to each member of the Gang of Four. Venice's box contained an exquisite silver pin; Corinne's a stunning scarf; Ollie's a silver bracelet engraved with Asian characters; Ian's a gold ring inlaid with a blue stone that perfectly matched his eyes.

"Funny how things work out, isn't it?" Corinne asked of no one in particular after they'd all exclaimed over Jeanne's thoughtfulness. For the plan had never been to get Martin appointed president of the company, only to get rid of Victor and April. But Harry Hsin knew a good thing when he saw it.

Corinne looked around the room — at her new boss and his wife, both of whom she adored; at Ollie, her fiancé, lover, and best friend; at Venice and Ian, two people who'd been strangers only two years ago but who were now like a brother and sister to her. *Maybe nice people don't always finish last,* she thought. *Maybe good boys sometimes win.*

The three couples sat, sipping their wine, until the door buzzer interrupted their reverie. Within ten minutes, the rest of the guests arrived, except one. Clive, Janet, Cal Ziotis, Meryn, and Gian all laughed and talked with their hosts as Martin worked the room, making sure no glass was empty.

Everyone was enjoying a third glass of wine when the door buzzer buzzed again. Corinne opened the door, and the new-comer was greeted with appreciative applause and cheers. He'd been integral to their plot; they couldn't have done it without him.

"Hello, Miss Jensen," Kaz Kazinski said, finding Corinne and kissing her on the cheek. "We're even. And you owe me a manuscript."

Corinne laughed. "Can I finish my wine first?"

"You want to capture it while it's still fresh in your mind."

"Don't you worry, Kaz. I have a good memory."

"And a diabolical little mind to boot."

"Thank you, but I can't take all the credit. It was a group effort."

"That's what I love about it. I'll have a publisher for you in no time."

"You think anyone will put two and two together?"

"No one'll know."

"Maybe I'll set it in San Francisco."

"No, New York is better. When do you start writing?"

"Tomorrow."

■ ■ ■ ■

EPILOGUE

■ ■ ■ ■

Mr. Kaz Kazinski
128 West 80th Street, Suite 3801
New York, New York 10025

Dear Kaz:
Well, here it is, as promised. Ollie, Venice, and Ian have read it, and they all like it. Venice didn't mind being turned into an Asian-American detective, and Ian is quite proud of his transformation into an architect. Ollie insisted on having a full head of hair, so his alter ego, Christos, sports a long luxurious ponytail. As for me, I've morphed into no-nonsense advertising executive Marcia Snodgrass. In Part One, we all meet for the first time when a con man rents us the same apartment. In Part Two, Marcia decides that her wicked boss and his evil secretary need to go, then conscripts her fiancé and two best friends into a fiendish plot to eliminate them.

I did a little something interesting with Part One — it has four possible outcomes, and the reader has to figure out which one really happened. By the time the reader gets into Part Two, though, all his or her questions will be answered.

Needless to say, this manuscript should not be submitted to any of my fellow editors at Clarendon & Shaw.

Things have been really wonderful here since Martin took over. The sun is shining again. The flowers are blooming. And we owe it all to you. Though, from what I hear, Harry would have fired Victor even if you hadn't offered to drop the lawsuit in exchange for HGSG getting rid of Mr. Jennings.

Stay well. Oh, and — burn this letter.

All best,
Corinne

P.S. A bit of good news to share: I've just been promoted to editorial director at C&S. See you at the wedding!

ACKNOWLEDGMENTS

I owe a debt of gratitude to many friends, all of whom assure me that they, too, want the apartment. I am particularly thankful to Marc Lieberman (screenwriter extraordinaire) and Lorraine Patsco for their encouragement and suggestions. For his help in the early stages, many thanks to John Sargent. For their sheer collegiality and superb advice, a hearty thank you to Bill Bognar and Tom Nery. For superb cover art, Stuart Dall. For his tenacity, a million thanks to my agent, B.C., who asked that he not be mentioned lest he be inundated with e-mails. A hearty twenty-one gun salute to the people at Ransom Note Press (Christian Alighieri, Emily Marlowe), who, unlike Victor Jennings, know how to run a publishing company. And, finally, love to the Partridge.

ABOUT THE AUTHOR

Steven Rigolosi is the director of market research and development at a Manhattan-based publisher of scientific books. *Who Gets the Apartment?* is his first novel. After years of living in Manhattan, he now lives in Northern New Jersey, where he is at work on future installments of the *Tales from the Back Page* series. His e-mail address is srigolosi@yahoo.com.

The employees of Thorndike Press hope you have enjoyed this Large Print book. All our Thorndike and Wheeler Large Print titles are designed for easy reading, and all our books are made to last. Other Thorndike Press Large Print books are available at your library, through selected bookstores, or directly from us.

For information about titles, please call:

(800) 223-1244

or visit our Web site at:

www.gale.com/thorndike
www.gale.com/wheeler

To share your comments, please write:

Publisher
Thorndike Press
295 Kennedy Memorial Drive
Waterville, ME 04901